Heathen's Creek

Haunted Love

Anna Hellström

To my loving husband Nicholas. Thank you for always supporting me throughout this writing journey, and encouraging me to fulfill this life long dream. I will always love you, you hold the key to my heart.

This is not a love story, some fates were destined moons ago.

Contents

Chapter 1

Decades passed; his deep longing for her stretched for eons—but now, it was only a matter of time.

Mia had always wondered if she had been here before, and moving back home would cause the memories to flood in. She didn't want to go back, but it was inevitable, and she dreaded the thought of the woman who materialized in the corner, in the mirror, and in her dreams, reentering her life. The fear of her presence loomed over Mia—a constant specter in her mind—no matter how hard she tried to push it away. Her identity was a mystery, her phantom-like form eerily pale. Her hair was always carefully styled, her waist cinched by a corset and fitted green velvet gown. A high lace collar rested snugly at her neck, a subtle hint that this ghostly figure may not have been from the present time.

The town itself had seen many generations, and Mia wondered if the woman had found her way from the cemetery, not eager to leave this earthly plane. In her youth, she had been fearful. Now, she felt uncertain. When she was young, the apparition would often startle her. The woman's piercing hazel eyes would closely follow her movements, her presence always lurking in the shadows, staring intently. She would stand brooding at her bedside as Mia slept, and on occasion, in the middle of the night, Mia would awaken not to the woman, but to the shadow of a monstrous animal at the foot of her bed. Anxiously rubbing her eyes, the visions would disappear, and she wondered—was the woman here to hurt her?

Mia wasn't sure, as the flashes of her appearance would arrive as quickly as they dissolved. She would appear in Mia's dreams, or in her day-to-day life, staring from a distance—no words ever spoken. Sometimes, when Mia was alone, she would hear her name whispered in various tones and voices, only to turn around and see no one there. Was this the woman? Or other spirits from the graveyard? She had never heard her speak before. As Mia grew older, she wondered if others could see her too, and the one time she asked her mother she was met with bewildered eyes, so Mia never brought it up again.

The apparition's presence left her confused, with occasional moments of déjà vu. Had she known her before? Were they related? As time passed, she tried to push aside her fear, ignoring the spectral figure and focusing on her life. And as she came of age and went off to school, the woman vanished from Mia's mind, until now.

As she looked out the window, the sun pierced through the hazy clouds, her long brown hair shined from the sky's rays, and her skin glimmered like moonlight. Taking in the nature surrounding her, she observed a wide array of brightly colored wildflowers, a breeze drifting through the tall grass, and the dense shadowy pine trees looming in the distance. Ten years had passed living in the city, and now she had moved back to her family home in Lavender Hill.

A college graduate, Mia had worked an administrative job at a record company—meaningful work she enjoyed, far removed from the realm of her youth. She was content, building a life of her own without the help of the old money she had grown up with. She was determined to live an existence far from the rich occupants of Lavender Hill, who spent their days drinking in endless glory, as life came so easily for them. That would never satisfy her. She knew her world would blossom far from Lavender Hill and the country-club conservatives she had always known.

Life in the city was going well for Mia—until one day, it wasn't.

Notified that the business was going under, devastation crawled through her skin as she could sense the world she had created fragilely shatter beneath her. She looked for work elsewhere, but luck was not on her side, and destiny began pulling her in other directions. One day, her mother called and asked if she wanted to come home, offering her the guest house to use as she pleased. Mia sighed in defeat. It wouldn't be a terrible option, she thought. *For it's my only one.*

Her father had passed away five years ago, and now her mother lived alone in the old three-story Victorian home Mia had grown up in. Handed down through several generations, her mother now owned the keys. When her father died, her mother had barely outwardly expressed her grief, keeping herself busy with as many hobbies as she could occupy, which included drinking her days away, playing tennis with Lavender Hill's high society, and spending the family fortune, which Mia wondered if there was anything left of. Her mother was clearly checked out and barely acknowledged that Mia had created a life of her own. They were from worlds apart, as Mia had always strived to be independent, away from the old money of Lavender Hill and its ancient occupants. And now, here she was—back in the withering town she had so desperately wanted to leave years ago.

The surrounding nature would give her some peace of mind, but she wondered what lurked in the shadows, or where her future would lead.

Her family home extended over several acres, predominantly made up of tall woods, the thick evergreen and pine always daunting her as a child, a shadowy black forest she could never see through. The family garden and array of wildflowers sprinkled near the home; it's creation long before she was born. A small guest house sat at the back of the property, its white paint now chipping from the weathered wood. Surrounding lavender bushes brought a sense of beauty to the old structure. The small purple petals swayed gently in the breeze against the decaying wood, and their heavenly scent wafted through Mia's nose each time she opened the guest house windows. She would make do—and make it her own, she thought to herself.

Turning away from the bedroom window, Mia picked up a large brown box and placed it on her bed to unpack her belongings. She had been home for a few days now, slowly unpacking and tidying up the dust and cobwebs that had accumulated over the years. Moments of sadness seeped into her mind as she missed what she once had, but she reminded herself—*it was only temporary*. She would find something to do. She knew her intuition would guide her where she needed to be.

She thought that today she would go into town and explore her old neighborhood, curious to see what had changed over the years. Grabbing her phone off of her nightstand, she texted her mother.

Going out for a few. Let me know if you need anything.

A quick response vibrated back.

Thanks, honey! I'm out for the day as well.

Placing her phone in her purse and grabbing her car keys, she was startled by the sound of an empty box falling off her desk. She turned around slowly, raising an eyebrow at the noise. *That's weird,* she thought cautiously. There wasn't a breeze in the room—the air was still, and she had closed the windows. Could it have been a mouse? she wondered, quickly checking the surrounding area. In the back of her mind, she knew the haunting history of Lavender Hill, but her rising anxiety tried to suppress the thought, locking it deep within. She had just moved back home and had no desire to deal with potential ghosts. *Must have been a breeze,* she tried telling herself confidently. Placing the box back onto the desk, she grabbed her belongings and headed into town.

Lavender Hill lived up to its name. A small town with fewer than a few thousand people, it sat on a mountainside overlooking the city. At its high altitude, the weather was usually cold, and the skies remained overcast. Lavender thrived throughout the area, and one could smell it from the heavens above. The decrepit town was mostly owned by old money, now withering away. The once neatly trimmed Victorian homes had become overgrown with weeds, as their owners were too old and frail to care for the lavish mansions, or had left for a warmer climate. To attract more youth and families, new housing developments had sprung up in recent years. Mia hadn't seen this newly developed side of Lavender Hill, and her growing curiosity compelled her to explore.

Getting out of her vehicle, her eyes adjusted to the familiar sights that had never changed. The central green park was still neatly manicured, and the red-brick buildings housed a variety of boutiques and small businesses. The circular fountain in the park still flowed effortlessly with crystal-clear water, stirring memories of her early youth spent splashing around in it. Now, she saw new families and children enjoying it as she once had. Walking down the sidewalk, she peered into the windows of the businesses Lavender Hill had recently gained. The old shop signs had been modernized, and she noticed an abundance of youthful-looking people walking around. Once predominantly occupied by an older generation, the town now attracted a younger crowd, as they had desired. A sense of satisfaction floated through Mia's mind, bringing a quiet hope that coming home had not been a mistake.

As she continued to observe her surroundings, walking past the endless windows filled with displays of boutique fashion, gifts, and bakery goods, her eyes locked onto a small sign that read Help Wanted. Above it, in blinking red neon letters, the shop name read JACK'S. Painted on the window in black lettering were the words: RECORDS + CD'S. She wasn't sure if it was a sign from the universe. She knew she was overqualified, but sharing her love of music was one of her favorite pastimes, and she certainly didn't want to spend her days at home with her drunken mother. Having had no luck finding work in recent months, this felt like a granted opportunity. She hesitated slightly, caught off guard by how quickly something had come along, but thought, *Screw it. Let's see what they have to say.*

High ceilings, walls plastered with band posters, and aisles filled with a vast collection of records—Mia's eyes lit up at the store's expansiveness. There was music in the air, and she liked what she heard. A sense of comfort settled in her chest; she could get lost in the music for hours.

Turning her head, she scanned the store until she realized the checkout desk was right beside her. A tall man, just over six foot, with dark shoulder-length hair, a clean beard, and an open blue flannel shirt looked up and smiled at her. She noticed his broad, muscular shoulders and the white cotton shirt underneath, defining his lean, athletic build. His features were smooth and handsome, lightening the grunge aesthetic he wore. He looked kind, as his white teeth sparkled towards her.

"Hi, can I help you with anything?" the man asked cheerfully.

He carefully looked her over, and she caught his eyes briefly scanning her body, the cut of her top subtly revealing skin, to which he seemed pleased.

She looked at him blankly for a moment, just realizing he had spoken.

"Oh, um... I'm sorry. I—I saw you have a Help Wanted sign outside?" she stuttered nervously.

Predominantly introverted, her words came out jumbled as nervousness bubbled up inside her. His eyes lit up at her question, his smile widening.

"Yeah, definitely! Are you looking to apply?" he asked eagerly.

She hadn't really thought about her future plans, but the opportunity had presented itself.

"Um, yeah. That would be great," she replied, offering an anxious smile.

The man looked elated by her response.

"Ok, cool! To be honest, we haven't had many people apply—or rather, *any*, actually—and I really need the help. You know, small town and all. Do you have any work experience?"

Mia looked at him, observing his joyful demeanor. She tended to remain calm, never exposing her internal anxieties, and admired people who were naturally enthusiastic. She laughed inwardly. *Yeah, I have work experience.*

"Yes, I do," she acknowledged, with a lighthearted chuckle. "I was doing administrative work for a record company in the city, but they closed down... so, I came back home. I can get you a resume if you'd like."

His eyes grew in surprise, clearly impressed by her corporate background. Then again, in a town like this, he probably was.

"Oh, then you're probably more than qualified. Here, let's go have a chat in the back and discuss some details. Right now, it's just myself and Lucy working." He pointed towards a girl behind the counter.

The checkout counter extended halfway down the store, and a girl with long blonde hair, red lipstick, and covered in tattoos was sorting records at the far end. As

Mia observed her, she noticed the array of piercings covering her ears and a hooped nose ring. She looked like a walking piece of art, and she looked tough. The girl glanced at Mia, giving her a thin smile and quickly going back to her task at hand.

He brought Mia to his back office, chatting with her about the shop and asking questions about her life. He seemed amused and remained charismatic, his eyes occasionally dropping from eye contact to take in her other assets. She didn't mind, though. He seemed kind enough, and far more fun than the corporate suits she had dealt with before.

"Well, if you have the experience you say you do, I'd love it if you could start on Monday. Would that be okay? I know it's only a few days from now, but we've been swamped, and I really need the help. Lucy will be here, and she can show you around. By the way, I'm sorry, did you tell me your name?"

"Oh, no, it's—uhm—Amelia. Er, it's... it's Mia. You can call me Mia. But yeah, that sounds great. I can make that work." Sweetly smiling, she felt hopeful and grateful for this new opportunity.

"Well, Mia, it's nice to meet you. I'm just going to have you fill out some paperwork, and I'll see you on Monday. My name is Jack, by the way." He reached his hand forward, the softness of his large hands shaking hers. He looked like a lumberjack, but his pretty-boy skin proved otherwise. His cologne, smelling of wood and musk, floated through her nostrils in his close presence. She was becoming keenly excited for the upcoming days working at his shop, amongst the music and these new people.

Looks like I've got a job.

That evening, as Mia lay in bed, her eyes glazed over, staring out the window into the shadowy moonlight and the stars sprinkled across the sky. Going over the day's events, she hadn't expected to get a job so quickly—let alone at a record shop. She relished the new experiences ahead, thanking the universe for this opportunity, thinking maybe luck was finally on her side. She thought of Jack and was strongly aware of his attractive physique. As her mind drifted, her heart started racing at the thought of him.

She hadn't dated in a few years, and a pinch of loneliness slipped into her mind as she imagined him slowly taking off his white cotton shirt, wearing nothing but his crisp blue jeans, and gently unzipping them in front of her. His broad chest would be gleaming with sweat, his hair lightly tousled as he stood before her. She felt warmth within, and her hand slowly made its way down her thigh when she was abruptly brought back to reality by the sound of a crashing thud at her bedside window.

Startled, Mia gasped. *What the hell was that?* Quickly getting up, she checked to see what had slammed against the glass at this late hour. *Maybe a bird?* she thought hopefully, knowing it could be anything out here in the woods of Lavender Hill.

Her pulse was racing as she slowly peered behind the curtains, but there was nothing—not even a scratch. The sound had been so loud she was certain it would've cracked the window, or at least left something lying below, but there was no sign of anything. *Was it all in my mind?* She looked up at the sky, curiously wondering if anything was there, but after a few moments, all she could see was a large bat flying in the distance. *It couldn't have been that.*

Maybe it was all in her mind, or nearby spirits trying to reach her. But instead of worrying herself over the frightening noise, she went back to bed, falling heavily into a dream, away from whatever had tried to startle her that day.

Chapter 2

He had forgotten how beautiful she was in person, the mere sight of her seemingly unreal—like a cruel, teasing joke sent from the stars above.

Monday morning arrived swiftly, and Mia stood in front of her closet, unsure of what to wear. The sky was overcast, signaling rain, and since her new job didn't require anything formal, she opted for something casual. A touch of makeup and a splash of red lipstick brightened her porcelain complexion, giving her cheeks a rosy shine. As her nerves bubbled up, she reassured herself this would be an easy transition—unlike her previous experiences. A funny, inner knowing told her this was the right move. It was where she was supposed to be, and everything would align for her.

When Mia entered the store, she noticed Lucy behind the counter, engrossed in her phone. The lack of customers gave the place an eerie silence, contrasting with the loud rock music blaring in the background.

"Hi!" Mia cheerfully greeted as she approached the counter.

Lucy put her phone down, recognizing who stood before her.

"Oh, hey girl! How are you? Ready for your first day?"

Despite her edgy appearance, Lucy's enthusiastic personality shined through. Mia wasn't sure what to expect, but she was immediately drawn to Lucy's outgoing nature.

"Yeah! What do we need to do?" she asked eagerly.

"Oh, it'll be easy," Lucy assured, dismissing any concerns with a casual wave of her hand. "There isn't too much to learn, and you'll pick it up quickly."

The hours flew by as Lucy showed her the daily tasks, such as ringing up customers at the register and organizing new products that came in each week. She explained how the store dealt with both new and used records and that people could come in to sell their old ones.

"We mainly need you to help sort out any new stock we get in and to help customers up front. Not so bad, right?"

"Yeah, I can do that," Mia nodded agreeably.

It was quiet for most of the day, and the girls spent their time chatting about their favorite bands and Mia's previous life in the city. Lucy, who Mia discovered was just a few years younger than her, had explained she grew up in a town close by. With the new developments in Lavender Hill, she had moved here two years ago.

"*I love it here,*" Lucy emphasized. "The town has really grown over the years, and there's quite a lot to do now. They even opened a music venue down the road, you should check it out sometime."

"Yeah, that sounds cool," Mia replied. This did pique her interest, as something of the sort was never available in town before. She recalled the numerous times her friends and her would sneak out and drive down the mountain to concerts in the city, only to find her mother waiting up for her at all hours of the night, boiling in anger.

As Lucy spoke, Mia quietly listened, struggling to keep up with the flurry of words that poured from her lips at a dizzying pace. The punk girl's stories seemed endless, and her rapid-fire enthusiasm made it difficult to follow. Yet, as Mia intently listened, that strange, inner knowing, funny feeling she'd felt earlier began to rise again. Her skin prickled with goosebumps and the hair on the back of her neck began to rise. She didn't know what was causing the chill within her, but she tried to focus on Lucy's words, until the punky blonde's eyes suddenly popped open in surprise, her mouth frozen mid-sentence.

"Oh fuck," Lucy whispered.

Mia looked at her questioningly, then followed her gaze.

He stood tall—nearly seven feet high. The long raven-colored tresses of his hair cascaded down his back, and his massive frame boasted bulging muscles, his powerful arms straining against the fabric of his black shirt. His face, perfectly carved and chiseled, resembled the epitome of masculine beauty, as if shaped by the ancient Norse gods themselves. His skin, pale as freshly fallen snow, contrasted sharply with his all-black ensemble. His crisp leather boots thundered across the floor as he walked past the girls, his darkened eyes meeting Mia's.

As their gazes met, the chill inside her deepened. Her mind froze under a feeling she couldn't name. She was struck by his stunning appearance—so beautifully crafted he looked like a work of art. His presence stirred a mix of wonder, trepidation, and reverence. She wasn't sure if she should be intimidated, in awe, or grateful to the heavens for bestowing such a uniquely handsome being upon her vision.

She stood motionless, transfixed, as he hurried to the back of the store. A whirlwind of emotions churned inside her. Drinking in his aura and his commanding presence, a profound sense of intrigue and mystery gripped her. The music that had filled her ears just moments before now faded into meaningless background noise, drowned out by her own racing thoughts. She simply froze, staring at him from across the distance.

"That's Everest Steele," Lucy whispered excitedly, snapping Mia back to reality. "Isn't he hot? He comes in like once a week or so to see if we have anything new. He's in a band—they're *so* good."

Slowly turning her head, Mia nodded in agreement. Her heart raced, her chest grew warm—his very presence stirring emotions she did not know she had within. How could someone have that effect with just a glance? She felt anxious. She felt nervous. But something wasn't right. His peculiar presence seemed almost ghostly, as if he arrived from another world. It brought up old memories and feelings of her encounters with spirits as a young girl.

"He's gorgeous," Mia muttered under her breath.

"What? Oh yeah, I know, right? But get in line, girl. We've all tried, and he won't budge. He's weirdly private about his life—I don't even know where he lives. Some girl though at one of his shows claimed she hooked up with him one time, but I think she was full of shit."

Mia's gaze remained fixed on him as he moved with quiet grace and poise through the store. His back muscles were visibly defined, even through the black fabric of his shirt, as he bent over stacks of records. His oversized hands delicately picked up each album, placing them back into their slots with care. For someone with such broad and heightened stature, he was careful in the way he moved and dealt with his surroundings.

She wondered if he was even human, but he had to be. *He certainly didn't walk in from the cemetery looking like that.*

The world around her seemed to slow down. Her heart pounded. Her thighs tingled in anticipation. Goosebumps rippled along her spine, the intensity of her emotions becoming overwhelming.

"You'll see him around if you like working here," Lucy added. "Sometimes he comes in and puts up flyers when his band is playing."

She pointed to the front entrance of the store, where numerous colorful flyers were stacked onto a bulletin board. Walking over, Mia browsed the vibrantly worded papers until one caught her eye—a bright orange flyer that read *VAMPIRIC HELL* in a scribbled font she could barely read. It reminded her of the covers of some of the metal records she had seen before. She pulled the paper off a tack to read the flyer, which listed only a date, address, and time that had already passed.

Lucy walked over to her and glanced down at the flyer she was holding. She nodded, tapping on it with her index finger.

"Yeah, that's him! We should go sometime."

Placing the flyer back up on the board, Mia turned to look at the beastly creature on the other side of the store. She couldn't tear her gaze from him, mesmerized by the width of his broad shoulders and the way his long, dark hair gracefully cascaded down his back as he carefully rifled through the records in front of him. Her heart was pounding, and an unfamiliar anticipation sent warmth flowing through her chest, leaving her breathless.

A small voice within her told her to go say hello, but she felt frozen in time, unable to move. She couldn't explain the feeling. While she did experience moments of nervousness or anxiety, this paralysis was unlike anything she had felt before. Unsure of what step to take next and engulfed in her thoughts, she was suddenly jolted out of her trance by a soft voice whispering in her ear.

"Go," it urged, the single word carrying a sense of purpose and certainty.

She shook her head, swiftly seeing that no one was around her. Lucy was back to texting on her phone.

What was that?

Momentarily unsure whether she had truly heard the voice, she took a deep breath and decided to walk towards the man, despite the surge of mixed emotions. *There has to be some explanation for this.* And as if spirit itself were on her side, a cold breeze blew past, nudging her forward. As she approached, the man's head slowly rose from the records, and he turned to face her.

As their eyes met, his expression quickly grew to one of concern, his brows drawing together sternly. A bony chill flowed through her being as she viewed him in his entirety, a fleeting wave of confusion and déjà vu rushing over her. Even from a distance, his eyes were black and dark, but she could feel a pull of electricity that ran beyond them. His furrowed brows betrayed a hint of hesitation, and then—just as quickly as he had appeared—his colossal footsteps left the store, a cold breeze blowing past her once again.

She stood frozen, even more perplexed now. Had she done something to upset him? She had merely tried to move closer, and yet nothing made sense. A deep, palpable tension lingered in the air, and her thoughts struggled to capture the inexplicable unease that settled over her.

Something was off. She could feel it. But the *why* remained a mystery. For now, at least.

"What was that?" Mia asked, dumbfounded.

Lucy looked up from her phone. "What was what?"

"You didn't see that? He gave me the strangest look and then ran out of here."

Lucy didn't bat an eyelash, shrugging nonchalantly. "Beats me, dude. He's weird." She chuckled. "He's hot, but he's not that friendly."

"Oh, that's too bad," Mia muttered quietly in disappointment. The wave of emotions washing over her was hard to decipher, but there had been something in his gaze—an intensity that hinted at more than him just being unfriendly. She could only wait and hope that the universe would offer some clarity. Or better yet, that she'd get the chance to confront the mysterious man, *Everest Steele*.

***

That night, Mia lay in bed, unable to sleep. She was still rattled by her encounter with Everest earlier that day. Her mind raced, trying to make sense of their brief interaction, wondering if she had somehow upset him. But why did her body still feel so strange—a mix of hot and cold, with confusion clouding her thoughts? She couldn't explain it, but the intensity of her emotions and the strange encounter with the mysterious man left her both uneasy and intrigued.

Maybe he is a ghost, she wondered, knowing how well the town of Lavender Hill was haunted by its cemeteries. She had never seen spirits while living in the city, which was part of why she had stayed away for so long. She'd read her fair share of ghostly tales and stories of unexplained phenomena over the years, but she couldn't quite put her finger on this one. So, she lay there, staring at the ceiling, her thoughts consumed by Everest Steele, silently hoping to cross paths with him again.

Suddenly, her heart leapt as a sharp rustling noise broke the silence in the corner of her room. Her body tensed, breath caught in her throat as she spotted a large rat rustling against a box, attempting to chew through. She *despised* rats. Though they often roamed the area, she had grown used to their occasional visits, as they also called Lavender Hill their home.

"So, it was you who caused all that commotion the other day," she muttered under her breath, finally succeeding in capturing the pesky rat in a box. However, its unusual silence sent chills down her spine. Bewildered, she cautiously peered inside—only to find emptiness staring back at her.

Confused and unsettled, she frantically searched the floor. There was no trace of the rodent anywhere. *Am I losing my mind?* The disappearance left her in disbelief.

As she stood up, a flood of ghostly childhood memories returned. Her heart dropped at the sight of the haunted woman—the same one from her past—her velvet green gown gently against the floorboards. Those piercing, emotionless eyes locked onto her, and an icy shiver ran down her spine. Though Mia had tried to bury the memory, locking it away in the recesses of her mind, it seemed inevitable that the woman would return—now that Mia had come home.

Mia felt the familiar grip of fear as the ghost appeared, but a new sense of anger coursed through her veins. She was no longer the helpless child. She demanded an explanation for this spirit's attachment to her.

But before she could speak—her chest heaving, her brows drawn in fierce determination—the woman vanished.

With frustration and exhaustion weighing her down, Mia cried out into the empty room, "Go away! Leave me alone!"

She climbed back into bed, pulling the covers tightly over her head. She knew the hauntings of Lavender Hill ran deep, and as she drifted into uneasy sleep, she reminded herself that she was in the spectral realm now. Though she had returned home, she was trespassing on *their* territory.

***

Over the next week, Mia quickly adjusted to her new job at the record store. The work itself was manageable, and most of the customers she encountered were pleasant and cheerful. She had the opportunity to meet several members of Lavender Hill's new generation, which was exciting, as her childhood memories predominantly consisted of spending time with people she thought were ancient. So far, she enjoyed her simple life back home—at least for the time being. Jack and Lucy were friendly, and she spent many of her days talking about and listening to music. In the back of her mind, though, she couldn't stop thinking about Everest. Her thoughts would drift, wondering when he would come back into the store, and what had made him rush out in haste?

As she stood behind the store counter, Mia noticed raindrops beginning to increase in size and intensity, plummeting to the pavement. A loud rumble echoed through the sky, followed by a violent downpour. A fierce storm had arrived, its wrath unleashed without warning.

Lucy groaned, resting her head against the counter with an exasperated expression.

"Great," she sighed, her shoulders slumping. "We're going to be stuck here all day with nothing to do."

Mia looked at her, a little surprised.

"Doesn't it rain all the time here? We're in the mountains." She laughed light-heartedly.

"Yeah, but it's storming now. It's not always this bad."

"That's true," Mia shrugged.

Time seemed to crawl by slowly as the morning hours progressed, and Mia and Lucy watched the continuous rain pour down from the gray sky. The occasional loud roar of thunder filled the air, as the sound of the rain blended with the rock music playing in the store. With nothing to do and no people in sight, Mia suddenly found herself filled with a sense of unease. Her heart began to race inexplicably, a strange intuition tugging at her mind.

Then—his heavy footsteps entered the store. She turned around to see who had arrived, and her eyes met his with sudden surprise.

As Mia nervously ran her hand through her hair, she was taken aback by the unexpected sight of him.

"Hi," she managed to utter, her voice trembling with a mixture of confusion and anticipation.

He cast a stern gaze in her direction for a moment, his nostrils flaring, his expression mirroring the same look of concern from their earlier encounter. His intense gaze seemed to pierce her soul, and she noticed that his eyes were an unusually dark shade, with a hint of red. He moved away from her, his leather boots thudding against the floor, echoing like the thunder erupting outside.

Lucy whispered into her ear,

"I told you, he's not that friendly."

Mia felt her cheeks redden with embarrassment. She had been caught off guard, and all she could muster was a timid greeting—now wishing she could sink beneath the floor.

"I think I should go talk to him."

Lucy looked at her pityingly, furrowing her brows.

"If you want to—but don't expect too much out of him."

Mia gathered her courage and managed to say,

"I'll be alright," though her words betrayed a bit of uncertainty. She was determined to at least attempt to engage with him, as he had been lingering in her thoughts all week long.

Despite the intense fear and nervous anticipation coursing through her, Mia took a deep breath and slowly approached him. Her heart pounded in her chest, and she could feel the pulsing of her blood racing through her veins, making her head spin. That soft, cold breeze was back, gently pushing her forward, guiding her closer and closer to him.

However, before she could reach him, she took one final, deep breath, trying to conceal the anxiety that was no doubt clearly etched on her face.

He was sorting through a stack of records, his colossal hands gently flipping through each one with careful precision. She found herself standing beside him, her nerves on edge as she took in the size difference between them. She felt small and vulnerable in comparison to the giant beast that stood before her.

"Finding everything okay?" she asked, tilting her head up towards him, her eyes observing the strong structure of his face. His height and robustly broad features made her feel as if she were looking up a mountain.

He looked down at her, his body stiffening as his dark red eyes locked onto hers, his face serious and stoic.

"What's your name?" he asked in a low, deep, rumbling voice that sent chills down her spine.

Mia was surprised by his question, her heart suddenly beating hard in her chest as she tried desperately to compose herself in the presence of this unearthly being.

"It's—it's Amelia, but people call me Mia," she hesitantly responded, continuing to gaze up at him, nervousness bubbling within.

He took in a long breath, his cold glare locked onto her doe-like eyes.

"It's nice to meet you, Amelia. My name is Everest."

The deafening energy in the air caused her nipples to harden, and her skin prickled in an arousal she had not felt in ages. He exuded an aura of power and strength, imposing and intimidating. And yet, his massive frame and dark gaze held a certain allure, bringing a sense of comfort she couldn't quite explain.

He looked at her momentarily, his brows narrowing.

"Do I know you from somewhere?" he asked.

Her eyes fluttered open, taken aback by his question. She swiped her tongue gently against her bottom lip, biting it in thought. She could see his eyes carefully observe her every move.

"Um, I don't think so? I just moved here recently."

Had she met him before? The more she thought about it, the more lightheaded she felt—a sense of déjà vu just around the corner, but it couldn't escape the depths of her mind, *yet.*

His response was cold, but she could detect a hint of disappointment in his gaze, as if something more was hidden beneath the surface.

"Oh. I see," he said.

"Is that why you walked away before?" Mia asked, her voice trembling slightly. "Have we met somewhere?"

She knew deep down that it was nearly impossible to forget a man of his stature—seven feet tall, dark and foreboding, yet undeniably attractive.

He shifted his weight back, momentarily uncertain as he contemplated his response. Mia was intrigued by the hint of trepidation in someone who otherwise radiated such strength. His intense gaze roamed over her, penetrating her senses. When her wide, doe-like eyes met his pools of blood, he gently touched her cheek before lifting her chin higher, bringing her attention directly to him.

In a tense whisper, he apologized,

"Sorry. I guess I must have... seen a ghost. It was... nice meeting you, Amelia."

Mia could see a hidden air of disappointment on him as he then briskly left the shop, leaving her once again in a fluttered state of shock.

Standing there bewildered and stupefied, she gradually turned around, trying to make sense of this mysterious man.

Was she to be offended?

Maybe Lucy's right—he is weird.

But as she walked back up to the counter, shaking her head in a state of distress, Lucy looked up from her phone.

"What happened?"

Mia shrugged, confusion written across her face.

"I—I don't know."

Chapter 3

He would never hurt her, for he knew far too well who she really was. He loved her, but he would have to make her realize she loved him too.

It was late in the night, and a blood moon shone brightly overhead, casting a reddish glow across the sky. Mia lay in bed, unable to sleep, her eyes wide open as she stared at the ceiling, her thoughts swirling in her mind. Several days had passed since her last encounter with Everest Steele, and his air of confusion and mystery left her flustered. Grabbing her phone off of her nightstand, she saw the time—it was nearly eleven. Feeling boredom creeping in, she decided, at this late hour, to go for a walk around the neighborhood. Without much thought, she slipped on her shoes and headed outside.

The air was humid and warm, with a light breeze carrying the fresh scent of pine and lavender throughout the area. Looking up, she saw the red moon glittering in the sky, big and luminous over Lavender Hill and beyond. As she walked down the block, the warm air clung to her face while a gentle summer breeze blew through her hair. The moon shone fiercely above, casting a soft light that illuminated the world around her, allowing her to navigate the darkness with ease. As she wandered through the quiet streets, she decided not to return home just yet and made her way toward the center of town.

Minutes passed, and she could see she was approaching the old, worn-down brick walls that made up most of the buildings in the area. As she strolled along the outskirts, she noticed the surroundings were unusually quiet. The only sounds being the soft whispers of the breeze and the subtle swaying of trees. Suddenly, her ears caught a high-pitched noise, and she froze in place. *Was that someone screaming?*

Cautiously, she approached the end of the brick wall, a sinking sense that something had happened—*or was happening*—just around the corner. Her curiosity getting the best of her, she slowly peeked her head around the corner, trying to glimpse what was going on.

Her chest tightened as her eyes widened in fear. She quickly ducked back behind the wall, gasping for breath as fear enveloped her. Though her thoughts were scattered, she gathered the courage to peek around the corner once more.

It was Everest—and a terrible scene unfolded before her eyes. She stared intently, taking in every detail. She noticed someone lying on the ground, lifeless and still, while Everest hunched over them. *Did he hurt them?* she wondered.

Accidentally stepping on a dry leaf, she winced as the eerie silence was broken. In an instant, his attention shifted. His gaze locked onto her. His breathing was ragged, and droplets of blood dripped down his chin. Her heart pounded as she stood paralyzed, locked in his intimidating gaze.

She let out a gasp of horror and quickly ducked behind the wall again. Her breathing turned rapid and uneven, fear surging through her as the only thought in her mind was to escape. She ran as fast as she could, bolting down the road towards her house, her mind spinning with confusion. In her panic, she accidentally made a wrong turn and ended up on a dirt path that led directly into the local cemetery. *Great, just my luck.*

Her heart thundered in her chest as she sprinted on, desperate to reach safety. But her path was suddenly interrupted when she tripped over a branch, and she found herself amidst the dilapidated, aged tombstones now surrounding her.

"Wait!" A heavy voice called out behind her.

Mia scrambled to her feet and turned around to see Everest approaching. Terrified, she stood unsure of his intentions, unsure of what he would do. Her chest heaved, and with every step he took towards her, the fear inside her grew. She stepped back until she hit a mausoleum wall. She was trapped. She couldn't move. Her heart felt like it was collapsing under the weight of fear—fear of the unknown standing in front of her.

Looking up at him, his towering presence overwhelmed her. His dark, shadowy figure was faintly illuminated by the moonlight, and his glowing red eyes locked intensely onto hers. Blood still trickled from his mouth. Frightened by what he might do next, she gulped, her heart pounding in her ears.

"Are—Are you going to hurt me?" she asked, her eyes wide with terror.

He stepped closer and studied her carefully, brushing the side of her cheek with his forefinger. Still silent, she stood there, drenched in anxiety, waiting for his response.

Her voice trembled as she pleaded, "Please don't hurt me."

He responded with a sly smirk, revealing sharp fangs. She realized he was a vampire, and her terror grew. *What's next, werewolves?* she wondered. Her breathing hitched in panic, her eyes widening.

He stood over her small, delicate frame, expressionless. As he gently caressed her cheek, she noted how cold his finger felt—like a winter's day. Closing the space between them, he lowered his head toward her neck.

"I won't hurt you, little doe," he muttered in a low, chilling voice.

He stared into her frightened eyes, but as she looked back, she saw something else behind that strong gaze—a feeling of anticipation.

"Don't you feel it too?"

"W-What?" Mia asked, confused.

She studied the mysterious familiarity of his face. A strange sensation of déjà vu washed over her. Despite her fear, a strange sense of security emanated from his touch, easing her initial trepidation. He knelt down, his height aligning with hers. Something deep within her stirred, compelling her to reach out and touch his cheek, caressing his cold skin before running her fingers through his soft, flowing hair.

He seemed to take pleasure in her touch, leaning into her hand with a quiet contentment. Arousal bloomed within her, heat growing between her thighs. Somewhere in the depths of her mind, a voice whispered, *This was meant to be. He's not going to hurt you.*

"I... think I do," she replied, her voice filled with hesitant wonder.

The red moonlight shimmered above them. He leaned in to nuzzle her neck, inhaling the sweet, floral aroma of her presence. His hands glided against her legs, gently gripping her thick thighs. As his cool breath grazed her neck, goosebumps paraded up her body. Unsure whether he was about to bite her or claim her, she felt a fire ignite within.

He tenderly kissed her neck, his fangs lightly grazing her soft skin, the blood of his kill smearing against her. A hot rush of wetness seeped through her core. He moved his head to catch her eyes, gazing down at her plump, red lips. Holding her thighs, he picked her up, her back pressed against the wall as he leaned in to kiss her. Her heart sank with intensity, as if she were weightless. She pressed into his wintry kiss, the icy sensation satisfying, as though she had known it before. She twined her arms around his neck, and he pressed his muscular chest against her, still gripping her thighs with great strength. Their lips unlocked, and his head nuzzled against hers. His breath sent a shiver through her as goosebumps danced across her skin.

His voice was low and silky as he murmured, "My little doe, such innocence and rare beauty... I assure you, I would never dream of hurting you."

He was a monster, but his soft, soothing words kept the flame growing within her. In that moment, her fear subsided, and her mind felt safe in his arms.

He gently guided her to stand, and a wave of ecstasy coursed through her body. She couldn't believe the reality of vampirism, but he exuded a sense of safety and solace, making her feel secure in his presence. As he kissed her, she didn't want to let go, wishing to remain in this moment of comfort and tranquility.

"Who are you?" she asked intently. "What do you want from me?"

His face grew cold and tense as he looked at her. Something was being left unsaid, and she was determined to find out. *Why can't he just tell me?*

"Amelia..." he whispered, his fingers weaving through her locks. He tilted her chin up towards him with gentle authority. "You may not recall me now, but I assure you, your heart will."

Stunned by his sharp response, something within his words caused her heart to warm tenderly. Whether or not he spoke the truth, she began to feel seduced by his being, wanting—at that moment—for him to kiss her again, no matter how strange and unusual the circumstance.

He acutely sensed the intensity of her emotions, his gaze darkening with desire as he knelt before her once again. His hands gently roamed her body, sending a wave of tingles racing through her. His voice was soft and deep as he uttered, "Let me show you," and she stood there, heart pounding, her anticipation mounting with every passing moment.

Lifting the thin fabric of her shirt, his hand lusciously cupped her perky breasts, flicking his thumb over her nipples as they hardened to his touch. Gently kissing her soft skin, she whimpered, her eyes lazily closing, head leaning back against the wall. His pressing kisses moved downward, his rough hands colliding with her skin as she relished the sensation of his touch. Her core was seeping wet as his hand dipped below her shorts, into the soft, warm folds of her delicate body, rubbing her sensitive hood. She let out a small moan, never having wanted someone so badly, the anticipation eating within.

In a single motion, his large hands effortlessly lifted her off the ground, gently laying her on the cool, damp grass of the graveyard. He swiftly removed her shorts, his gaze filled with voracious desire to savor the sweet taste of her nectar.

Waves of ecstasy washed over her as he softly kissed her inner thighs, his touch sending tingles through her entire body. She wasn't sure whether this was real or just a dream, but she tried to push away the doubts and lose herself in the sensations, his tender touch creating an intimate atmosphere in the graveyard, the soothing scents of pine and lavender drifting around them.

The touch of his tongue was just as cold. Her chest rose as she bit her lip in surprise. Circling her tender core, she moaned in pleasure at the soft graze of his fangs and his breezy breath that paraded into her being, giving her moments of bliss she had never known before. He lapped her up—lovingly, lusciously, and lustfully—drinking in her nectar as she bucked against his face, wanting everything he could give. He sucked on her swollen pearl, his thick digits sliding into her wetness. Her body tightened with an onslaught of intense pleasure, causing her eyes to flutter shut in delight.

In the midst of her bliss, quick, fragmented images surged through her mind—faint memories of a past life. She saw a quaint little wooden home, a sun-kissed field, and the vampiric figure of Everest Steele walking towards her. Through these swift glimpses of another time emerged a vision of herself wearing a green velvet gown, standing in front of a mirror. To her astonishment, the reflection was not her current self but the ghostly image of the Haunted Woman.

Startled, her breath caught in her throat, momentarily breaking her away from the wave of bliss. Confusion mingled with the visions, leaving her baffled by the inexplicable imagery. Everest continued to gently kiss her body until the wintry breath of the vampiric man met her plump, rosy lips, the sheen of her orgasm still upon his mouth.

With his lips tracing a path along her skin, he whispered between soft, intoxicating kisses, a sly smirk curving on his lips. "Now, do you remember?" he murmured, his voice dripping with sultry smoothness.

Chapter 4

He would not let too much time pass before see-ing her waking beauty again. The quiet des-peration in his heart bled with pain, yearning for her to remember who she was and where she came from.

"You look awful."

Mia looked up from sorting records to see Lucy standing above her, arms crossed, leaning against one of the stacks.

"Yeah, thanks," she muttered, placing a box down and rising to her feet. "I'm just tired," Mia sighed.

The events from the night before had left her confused and uncertain. She couldn't tell if it had all been a strange dream or a new reality she now had to accept. As her mind wandered back to the previous night, she remembered him leaving her behind amidst the graveyard, forcing her to question the validity of her experience. As he departed, a large bat flew overhead and disappeared into the distance. *He's a vampire.*

She remembered him softly kissing her, his deepened voice whispering tender words—promising to return *soon*. But then there were her orgasmic visions of the Haunted Woman. *It must have been a dream,* she thought, trying to convince her fragile state of mind. Yet her subconscious knew otherwise.

"Uh-huh. What did you do last night?" Lucy nudged her shoulder, her voice eager.

"I just... I had a late night, that's all," Mia replied quickly, shutting her down. It was too much to handle, and divulging such a monumental secret felt risky. How could she explain that vampires existed? She feared Lucy would question her sanity—or worse, think she'd lost her mind and risk losing her job. She liked working at the record shop and didn't want to take that chance.

Yeah, vampires are real. Shit, I hope it was just a dream. Full moons do that, right?

"Right," Lucy said slowly, skepticism creeping into her voice as she eyed Mia. It was clear she didn't believe her, but Mia was too weary to explain any further.

"Well, anyways, did you hear that some woman was killed last night over near Orchard Street?"

Oh no. It was all real.

Mia's eyes widened as she slowly turned her head towards Lucy. "Wha—what?" she stammered cautiously. If it was the same woman she'd seen lying in the road, then it hadn't been a dream. Everest *is* a vampire—and she *did* hook up with him in the graveyard.

"Yeah, apparently some old lady was found dead over there this morning. Just lying in the road, bleeding. Not sure what happened."

Mia's eyes narrowed, anxiety flooding within. "That's terrible!" Guilt was already churning in her stomach. She knew what had happened but explaining that vampires are real would make her sound insane, *and the fact that she witnessed a crime.*

Lucy shrugged. "Eh, it happens. Between you and me, I've noticed over the years there've been reports of people showing up dead in some of the neighboring towns, but it's always some crazy person or someone pretty old. It's only like once in a blue moon, though." She added with a grin, "Maybe there's a serial killer targeting them or something."

Mia stared at her blankly, her heart pounding as dread settled in. "Yeah... maybe." She wasn't sure how to explain what she had seen. She trusted Lucy to some extent, but they weren't particularly close. She didn't want word of her encounter with Everest to spread.

I'm so screwed.

Her mind wandered as she looked down, biting her nails. When she glanced back up, Lucy was already texting, absorbed in another conversation. *She has the attention span of a mouse.*

"Can I ask you something, though?" Mia asked cautiously. She wasn't sure about discussing Everest, but Lucy seemed to know more about the current state of Lavender Hill and its occupants. She might have some information to share.

"Yeah, what's up?"

"This might sound kind of silly," Mia began hesitantly, "but have you ever heard of anything... lurking in the woods here?"

"What?" Lucy gave her a strange look.

"Yeah, like... I don't know. When I was a kid, I'd see ghosts sometimes in the cemetery, but no one ever believed me. You know, things like that?"

Lucy pondered for a moment, then a knowing smile appeared on her face. "Oh... yeah, I think so. Now that you mention it, this guy came in once and told Jack and I he saw a werewolf up in the hills. We just laughed at him because of how crazy it sounded."

Mia's face fell with disappointment.

"But I definitely think there are ghosts around. This place is haunted as shit," Lucy continued, her eyes widening as a new thought occurred to her. "Oh fuck, do you think something hurt that old lady?"

Mia stumbled over her words. "Well I... no. I... I just wanted to know if you had heard any stories before."

The excitement dimmed in Lucy's eyes as she shrugged. "Oh. Well, no, not really. At least not that I know of. But I wouldn't be surprised. There's always weird shit going on around here."

"But do you believe in that kind of stuff?" Mia asked, hopeful that she might find one person who could be an ally.

"Well, yeah, I guess? I mean, anything is possible. I wouldn't be surprised if we found out Sasquatch has been living up in the hills this whole time."

Well, that wasn't a no. So that's promising.

"Why are you asking about this?" Lucy raised an eyebrow. Mia, feeling both anxious and determined to remain calm, tried her best to look composed. "Have you seen something?"

"No... no, not recently. I just, uhm... I don't know. Like I said, I've seen ghosts around and didn't know if it was just me, that's all."

For a moment, Lucy looked at her curiously but softened with a smile. "You're good, dude, don't worry. You know you can tell me anything, right?"

"I appreciate that, thanks," Mia replied with a thin smile, turning back to her work. Despite her efforts to focus, her mind remained preoccupied with the events of the previous night. A part of her longed to see him again, but a deep sense of confusion and anxiety pulled at her—leaving her feeling conflicted.

***

Exhaustion weighed heavy as Mia collapsed into bed the moment she got home. Too overwhelmed to think, she dove beneath the cool covers, hoping anything of a haunted nature would leave her be, at least momentarily.

As the hours passed and the night grew on, a storm brewed overhead. Thunder rolled through the sky, rousing her from sleep. Her eyes shot open as sharp bolts of lightning flashed behind her linen curtains. She rubbed her eyes as the thunder boomed louder, a crash of lightning dove down, and with it, the tall shadow of a man standing at the window amongst the pouring rain. Who could it be, but the monstrous *Everest Steele.*

Gasping with a fright, Mia did not know who stood beyond the window, assuming it was either the shadows that be or a killer of the woods. She quickly darted up and parted the curtains, her eyes widening as she spotted him. Standing there—tall and muscular—his dark hair whipping in the storm's furious winds, rain pelting down on him. His clothing clung tightly to his damp skin; the fabric plastered against his sculpted frame. He had come back for her, yet this vampiric man of mystery once again caught her in a fright, right from a deep sleep. His dark eyes lay upon her, hungrily grasping for her touch once again, and she felt a warmth in her chest that intensified.

How did he know where I live?

Opening the window, the lashes of rain angrily poured onto her, and she squinted against the heavy winds.

"Would you like to come in?" she yelled over the thunderous storm.

His stony face carefully nodded, and the vampiric beast wasted no time crawling in through the window, out from the darkened storm.

He could've used the front door, she curiously thought as she watched his large frame unfold through the window.

Her heartbeat quickened as she looked up at his giant stature before her, feeling quite small amid the cozy bedroom. Somehow, he knew where she lived—and yet she let him in. Her inner consciousness knowing she would be safe in his presence. He moved towards her, his eyes radiating a deep red as they wandered over her body, sculpted beneath her silk nightgown. She felt his cold breath against her skin, sending shivers up her spine, and her core clenched in anticipation.

"I need you, little doe," he murmured possessively, closing the space between them. "You are for me and no one else."

His rough fingers traced along the supple skin of her arm, leaving gentle trails of goosebumps in their wake as her flesh quivered beneath his touch. She was entranced, lost in the depths of his dark, fiery eyes, feeling a growing desire for more of his touch—his embrace. She didn't understand what was happening, but that funny, inner knowing told her this was meant to be, and she felt safe in his presence. Her heart raced, pounding loudly in her ears, and she wondered if he could hear its quickened rhythm.

As his body pressed against hers, Mia could feel the bulge beneath his denim jeans pressing into her, the thick swell aching to come out and play. He leaned in for a gentle kiss, and the sharp graze of his fangs collided against her tongue, his kisses moving down to her chest as the rough texture of his fingers flicked over her hard nipples.

He was hungry. Taking her small body, he threw her onto the bed, a shocking thrill of excitement fluttering through her. He bent down, rucking up her satin night-gown to expose her beautiful core, letting out a low growl of satisfaction. His large hands smoothed over her curves, squeezing her thighs, spreading them wide, and trailing kisses towards her entrance. Her body reeled in pleasure at his every touch, and as she felt his lips nearing her entrance, she tensed at the wintry delight of his cold breath.

As his tongue entered the pink lips of her sex, her breath hitched, and he kissed her soft folds, swirling his tongue around the precious pearl he now claimed. Mia closed her eyes, her sharp nails tightly gripping the soft fabric of her duvet, losing herself in the pleasure he so actively gave her. Every movement of his mouth and swirl of his tongue made her moan blissfully. She writhed and bucked her body closer to him, feeling herself come to a climax. As she yelled his name against the thunderous sound of the storm, a strike of lightning flashed outside. Her nerves tensed as a sprinkle of stars came pouring out, her orgasm flinging her into a realm of dreams. She was mesmerized in her ecstasy, and he continued to gently kiss her inner thighs, holding onto them tightly.

"My Amelia," he muttered deeply, his lips shining with her sweet nectar. His eyes locked onto hers, a spark of ownership flaring within. He had claimed her, but he wasn't done yet. There was still more of her he wanted, more of her that needed to be made his own.

Mesmerized by the intensity of his gaze, she couldn't think outside the realm of pleasure she was now in.

He stood tall and dominant before her, his muscular body on full display. As he slowly slipped off his damp shirt, the dim light from the storm played upon his chiseled frame, creating an alluring silhouette. Biting her bottom lip, Mia had never seen such a beautifully sculpted specimen—at least not in the flesh. But what truly sparked her excitement was the moment he unzipped his jeans. Exposing his hard cock, it sprang free, his balls full and aching for release.

"Is... is that for me?" she questioned softly, a hint of apprehension in her voice. Her eyes slowly trailed up his imposing figure until they met his intense gaze.

He smirked, a thin smile forming on his mouth, but the fire within him only grew stronger. Slowly, he grabbed his shaft in hand, stroking it in front of her. His head lowered, and the long strands of his black hair fell over his face.

As he brushed his hair aside, Mia noticed the taut cords of his forearms flexing with the gesture. Speaking almost tenderly, he murmured, "Oh, little doe, it has only ever been for you."

Mia was unclear of his words, but her inner knowing knew truth to it. At this moment, the wetness inside her wanted to seep out, a hunger within wanting him inside of her.

Leaning down for a kiss, his large frame overpowered her, and his hard erection smoothed against the wet lips of her sex. She moaned at his touch, bucking her hips eagerly, desperately wanting his every thrust.

"My Amelia..." he murmured, low and hoarse, the words muffled by his kisses, his lips brushing her skin as she felt the curve of his smile. "Such a needy girl."

"Don't you want it too?" she quietly breathed, her chest rising with anticipation.

His kisses abruptly stopped. His cold eyes slowly turned towards her, and his hand gripped her jaw. She could feel the thickened head of his cock positioned at her entrance as she looked into his serious gaze, unable to move from his grasp.

"I have always wanted you," his deepened voice said, serious and filled with intensity.

And in that moment—taking his cue—he thrust into her, the force of his hard erection making her gasp, a rush of pleasure pouring in.

He claimed her mercilessly, the beast within him powering his thrusts with a desire that had not been released in over a hundred years. Mia writhed and moaned as he worked her cunt, his cock soaked in her wetness, whispering words of dominant affection that sent tingles up her spine. Her lips pressed tightly against his smothering kisses, and her sharp nails raked across his defined back as she screamed his name in desire. Her inner walls pulsed around the thickness of his shaft, and as her eyes closed, nearing her climax, every thrust was once again struck by a wave of surreal visions.

Images flashed: herself in a small cabin filled with the scent of apple pie and burning wood. She saw glimpses of her hand being held by larger, rougher fingers, a ring slipped onto her slender digit. Then, as she looked up, there *he* was—gazing down at her with an expression of deep affection and tenderness.

As her nerves electrified, a sensational rush coursed through her, her orgasm tearing free just as a strike of lightning flashed beneath her eyes. With several more thrusts, Everest groaned against her ear; his chilling seed spilled into the warmth of her cervix, their sweating bodies meshed into a state of bliss.

Mia slowly opened her eyes; her gaze directed towards her bedroom mirror. For a fleeting instant, there she was—a flash of the ghostly woman right before her. Not having time to clearly adjust her sight, the apparition rushed forward, an icy current slamming into Mia's mind, causing a sickening vertigo to grip her soul.

Everest spoke with unwavering determination, his words like a soft but powerful command. "Now do you remember, my Amelia? You belong to me," he murmured, his breath caressing her ear and igniting a subtle shiver. As she fought off the dizziness, struggling for control, her hand instinctively reached out, running through his damp hair. In that moment, something shifted within her. The realization that she knew him was a flicker of recognition, a spark in the depths of her subconscious.

"I believe I do know you," she whispered, her voice filled with a mix of fascination and uncertainty.

He was quietly elated by her words, a reddened sparkle appearing in his eyes. It was destined to occur, he understood—knowing that she would eventually give in. He would make it happen. Their souls were always predestined to reunite. Though the timing had never been clear, here she was, over a century later, her radiant soul having taken shape in someone new. She was irrevocably his, and he could feel the bonds of recognition strengthening between them.

She understood the universe worked in mysterious ways and had always relied on her intuition. A believer in magic and the unseen, she accepted that her situation, while shocking, was not beyond the realm of possibility. The idea of past lives always held a thread of truth for her. The realization that the apparition haunting her was a reflection of her own soul made sense now. She had spent most of her life running from the ghostly woman. Still, she wondered if this was Everest's doing—if his vampiric essence had sent the specter to her so she would always find her way back to him. *It didn't matter now, she thought.* She couldn't change the ties of her soul to his. This was where she was meant to be. Whether she had a choice in the matter or not, in this moment, she felt safe and comfortable in his arms.

In the presence of his fearsome yet comforting figure, she felt a surge of warmth in her chest, as cold as he may be. She closed her eyes to rest, falling into a state of blissful surrender as he lay beside her, gently running his fingers through the long strands of her hair.

Her body felt frail. She wheezed and coughed, the bed creaking with every small movement. The sun shone brightly through the windows. Outside, she could see a stream running by, hear birds chirping, and feel a breezy wind stirring the world. As beautiful as the countryside was, she had never felt worse—her body slowly breaking down, the illness inside her still unnamed.

He came to her bedside, exhaustion and stress lining his face, bringing grim news. The doctor couldn't help anymore—but maybe this woman could. At this point, they were willing to try anything. As the weeks passed, her body grew more and more frail, unable to move, unable to eat. He said he would be back in a day, hopefully with help, hopefully with a cure.

Her bony hands tightly grasped his, still full of life and hope. He placed a kiss upon her dry lips, his eyes filled with worry. He left her there with many promises of a brighter future, his last words being I love you. *She would love him in every lifetime, dearly hoping she would survive this illness to spend the rest of her days with him.*

The witch in the woods—*that's who he was told to find. Several hours from town, the journey was long, but he rode with urgency. His horse could only move so fast, but as nightfall came, he reached the rotting cabin, tucked away deep within the trees. A thin curl of smoke rising from the chimney gave him hope that someone was home who could help.*

The woman must have sensed his arrival, as before he placed his feet upon the earth, she opened the door. Enticing in demeanor, she looked youthful—her blonde hair swept down her back, a black lace dress trailing to the ground and beyond. Her eyes sparkled and intensified as he drew near.

She welcomed him in, her red lips smiling graciously, repeatedly commenting on his handsome appearance. As he explained his situation, she nodded sympathetically, smoothing a hand over his in a gesture of comfort. As beautiful and endearing as she appeared, his mind quickly turned to darkness. Maniacal laughter echoed through his ears as his heavy body fell to the floor—and that's all it took to forever change him.

He woke up, unsure if hours or days had passed, dimly seeing sunlight through her darkened curtains. Crouching before him, she smiled, sharpened fangs pronounced within her mouth. He was horrified, though a bruising pain throbbed in his head, the source of which he couldn't understand. She handed him a cup, a dark liquid swirling within, explaining that he must drink it to feel better. He hated this woman already, but would do anything to rid himself of the searing pain tearing through his body. He drank quickly; the liquid tasted of thick iron, a metallic tang he nearly spat out.

"Such a handsome man you are," the witch cooed, caressing his black hair and eyeing him thirstily. "Couldn't let a man like you go to waste."

Unsure of her meaning, he felt terrified. With all his strength, he stumbled upright, quickly fleeing the witch's house. A sharp sting pulsed at his neck while his head pounded with relentless pain. His fingers brushed along the side of his throat, coming away with blood smeared on the pads of his digits.

But it was already too late. The evil witch had turned him. Too much time had passed, and when he finally burst through the door of his own home, she lay there quietly—her soul long gone, breath having left her days before. He had now lost his love and been made into a monster.

Mia was suddenly jolted from her sleep, her body drenched in sweat, chest heaving with each breath. She frantically scanned the room, eyes wide with alarm as she grasped her surroundings. The storm still raged outside, its thunderous roar shaking the air. She looked beside her, and there was Everest, watching the storm with a calm, stoic expression on his face. *That's right, vampires don't sleep.*

Fear gripped her as she looked at him, but he slowly turned his gaze towards her, his expression composed. He silently took her hand in his, a gentle gesture meant to soothe her frayed nerves. Though she couldn't be certain, her intuition whispered that he knew about her dream. Whether it was the product of her mind or a result of the vampiric man's influence, she did not know.

Placing his hand on her cheek, he guided her face towards him and kissed her softly, his elongated fangs brushing against her lips. "Now you know, little doe," he murmured through pressing kisses.

As the memories of her previous life flooded her mind, her heart ached for his touch. Ripples of pleasure coursed through her where his hand caressed her skin. She wondered if he would turn her. Had her soul waited all this time simply to be reunited with him? Or did he want her to remain in this mortal form? She hadn't given much thought to that possibility yet.

"I must go. The sun will rise soon," he stated, a note of unease in his voice. She nodded, quietly noting the small facts she had learned of vampires over the years were true. *Drinks blood, no sun, doesn't sleep.*

Mia watched him get dressed, admiring the movement of his muscles with every twist and turn. His long black hair swept over him as he reached down to pull on his jeans. *He's mine?* It was a wonderful yet terrifying thought. Every woman in town would envy her—if they knew. But at any moment, his inner vampire could tear the flesh from her neck. Was she to be so lucky?

"I will come for you in several days," he commanded in a low voice, sitting on the edge of her bed and firmly taking her hand. "I want you to pack a bag. You'll be coming to my place this weekend."

She nodded obediently, fully aware that she wanted to see him again. Still, a lingering sense of dread crept beneath the surface. Did she even have a choice? Her mind wandered to dark possibilities—visions of being whisked away into the woods, axed off, or having her neck bitten like the old woman in town. *Calm down, Mia. He would never do that.*

"Where do you live?" she asked, curiosity overcoming her hesitation. She longed to understand more of this beastly vampire.

In his true Everest fashion, he did not explain himself, keeping his air of mystery wrapped tightly around him. "I will show you. It's not far."

He kissed her goodbye, the wintry chill of his breath grazing into her lungs as she took him in one more time. The aching pressure in her heart hoped he would return sooner rather than later. What a terrifying secret this was to be—but the thrill of a new life sparked a quiet excitement within her.

Taking his leave, he scaled down from the window, and she rose to ensure his safe descent through the rain. She stood there, watching him disappear—just like all the other apparitions and creatures that lurked in the murky shadows of Lavender Hill. The rain fell heavier still, the scent of pine and lavender thick in the air as she contemplated the uncertain path ahead of her future.

Chapter 5

He would take her to his domain, where the darkened comforts of his world put ease in his chest. He hoped she would also find pleasure in his shadowy realm, for he would never let her go.

"What the hell am I going to wear?" Mia quietly mumbled to herself as she rummaged through her closet. A hint of uneasiness crawled through her chest, but her intuition reassured her she would be fine.

He had never given her a time to be ready by, and the morning sun was beginning to hide behind the afternoon's dark gray clouds. Noticing a pattern of his absence during sunny days and his appearance under overcast skies, she assumed he would arrive later that afternoon. Settling on a black silk dress, she paired the outfit with leather boots and red lipstick.

An hour had passed. As she sat at her vanity, her long red fingernails drummed against the desk. The sight of light rain caught her attention, and she opened the window, taking in the familiar scent of the sky's tears and the surrounding nature. Inhaling deeply, she filled her nostrils with the fragrance of wet earth and pine, and the sound of water lightly pouring onto the ground flowed through her ears. It was peaceful. As she relished in the quiet nature of her home, a breeze began to blow, her hair sailing into her face as she pushed it aside—and in that moment, a large black pickup truck drove down the road, turning into her driveway.

She wasn't sure what to expect. It was never noted in her storybook tales that vampires could drive. How he managed to even find a vehicle that fit his colossal frame was beyond her. Alas, the old truck rumbled down her driveway, and there he was—his imposing stature unfolding from the chunk of metal as he stepped out, eyeing her beauty through the open window, desire glowing in his gaze.

She smiled, noticing the red glow of his eyes fixed on her. "A truck, huh?"

He smirked, a sly smile tugging at his mouth as he chuckled at her comment. Nodding in satisfaction, he said, "Come, let's go."

Grabbing her bag and a jacket, she locked up the house and headed out on her new adventure—wherever that may be.

***

As he held the car door open for her, she looked up at him, a hint of anxiety in her eyes.

"Do I look alright?" she asked, a touch of apprehension in her voice.

He noticed the concern on her face, his nostrils flaring slightly. "You look beautiful, Amelia," he reassured her, his giant hand wrapping around the small of her back and drawing her closer. "There's no need to worry, little doe," he whispered against her lips, his touch working to soothe her nerves.

Mia looked into his darkened eyes, how quickly they turned crimson in his heated desire. Yet her inner knowing felt safe in his gaze of a bloodened sea. Was he hypnotizing

her, or were her past-life instincts giving her the reassurance she needed? Whatever the case, she smiled into the
comfort of his pressing kiss, then climbed into the old
black truck.

The drive to his mysterious home was significantly
longer than Mia had anticipated. He had assured her it was
only a short distance away, but as they continued traveling, the journey felt endless. They drove up hills, through
bends, and then some. Thirty minutes passed, and Mia
began to question if they were even going in the right
direction.

Shit, maybe he is going to kill me, she quietly wondered. *Maybe he's been trying to lure me in this whole time.
He could bite me in the woods, and no one would ever find
me.*

"Where are we going? I thought it was close," Mia asked
hesitantly.

Everest noticed her nervous demeanor and ran his hand
up and down her thigh, the warmth of his touch gently
calming her frazzled nerves.

"We're nearly there, little doe," he murmured softly.

He remained mostly silent for the majority of the drive,
as was his usual manner. He tended to convey thoughts
and feelings through gestures and body language, his strik-
ing vampiric presence speaking volumes for him. She as-

sumed he possessed some psychic abilities, given what she'd gathered from movies and literature, and it appeared that his powers did indeed lie within the realm of the mind. Over time, she'd come to believe he had used those abilities within her dreams, showing her visions of what her soul already knew. They barely knew each other—*in this lifetime*—yet the more time she spent with him, the more she felt a comforting presence that all was true. She did know him before.

Maybe, she thought as she stared out the window at the thickening forest, he would open up more once she entered his world.

Another twenty minutes passed, and they turned onto a narrow, winding dirt road that seemed to swallow the vehicle whole. The thick, towering evergreens blotted out the sky, leaving only a few sparse glimpses of dimming blue light. The uneven road was nearly consumed by darkness, the truck bouncing and jolting as it cruised along the gravel path.

As they rounded a corner, the densely packed trees abruptly gave way to a clearing. A green hill appeared out of the thicket, and an old, rusting wrought-iron gate stood at its top. Heavy chains and a thick, sturdy lock had been wrapped around it, securing the barrier tightly shut.

"Hold on," Everest mumbled, stepping out of the vehicle to unlock the gate.

Mia watched him closely as he pulled out a key to open the padlock.

"Where are we?" she asked, eyes narrowed as he stepped back into the truck.

"We're almost there, little doe," he said soothingly, his hand gliding gently over her thigh as the journey continued.

He was right. Within minutes, they pulled into a short dirt driveway, where a large black wood cabin stood upon a grassy hill. The building was impressive, with high rooftops and stained-glass windows, and two fearsome gargoyles perched high above its entrance. Their stone faces were set in anger, as if to ward off intruders. Evergreen trees scattered below as far as the eye could see, stretching off into the distance. Wildflowers dotted the landscape, their bright hues contrasting with the tall grass that surrounded the dark home.

Mia was struck with awe as she stepped out of the vehicle to take in the scenic surroundings. He lived in a place that seemed almost like a fairytale—vibrant foliage beneath the darkening sky, and a daunting structure wrapped in shadows. The air was crisp and clean, and the only sound was a soft, gentle breeze.

She turned to look at him, her face lighting up with a pleasant smile.

"It's beautiful," she whispered.

Amused by her delight, his lips twisted upward in a thin smile. "Come," he said, reaching his hand out for hers. Her small fingers entwined with his oversized digits. As they walked towards the front door of his home, Mia took special note of a large goat grazing nearby. Its coat was a rich, velvety black, with long, black horns that curved gracefully against its skull. The goat slowly lifted its head, its gaze fixed intently on hers. For a moment, the animal seemed almost mythical—its presence powerful, its eyes locked on hers with intensity.

"You have a goat?" she asked curiously.

He paused to rummage through his pockets and retrieve his keys, then nodded with a slow smile. "Yes, that's Billy," he affirmed, his eyes drifting towards the goat, who had returned to the grass and resumed grazing.

Still watching the animal, Mia studied the goat closely. She couldn't explain it, but she suspected there was more to Billy than initially met the eye.

Mia's eyes widened in awe as she stepped into the realm he inhabited. Everything, from top to bottom, was swathed in black. He had mentioned that he built the residence himself, tailoring it to fit his towering frame with tall ceilings and expansive rooms. In a previous life, he had been a man of many trades—skilled in welding and forging—a man of *steel*. He had constructed a home to suit his needs and desires, one that reflected his affinity for the shadows.

The interior of the home was adorned in shades of dark blue, gray, and red, reminiscent of the Victorian era. The décor, familiar and nostalgic to him, consisted of furniture crafted from black wood and soft velvet, all set against darkened floors. The lighting was kept low, with numerous candelabras strategically placed throughout the house, their thick candle wax seeping down their sides. The home possessed a haunting, eerie aura, yet Mia appreciated the intricate craftsmanship of this handcrafted dwelling.

He took her hand again and led her down a dimly lit hallway, where faint sounds of music and conversation could be heard. In the distance, she noticed the sound of drums suddenly ceasing and a voice pausing to ask a question. As they entered the room at the end of the hall, Mia found herself inside a music studio, where three towering figures stood before her, their long hair framing their faces.

The men immediately halted their music upon hearing the door open. Their gazes shifted towards the entrance, spotting Mia beside Everest. A hush fell over the room as they laid eyes on the human before them.

"Guys, this is Amelia," he said assertively, his arm wrapped possessively around her waist as he drew her closer.

A palpable tension filled the room as they all acknowledged her presence with nods. Mia couldn't help but notice the intense red glow emanating from the eyes of one of the men, confirming his vampirism. An uneasy thought slipped into her mind—*could she be their dinner?*

"Tommy, cut that shit out!" Everest snapped.

The man holding a bass quickly shook his head, the desperate look of thirst disappearing instantly.

"What the fuck are you doin', man? You know who she is!" one of the other men yelled with a strong East Coast accent. With the back of his hand, he swiftly slapped the man's arm.

"Sorry, I, uh... I don't know what came over me," the man on bass—*Tommy*—rubbed his head in confusion.

"I'm sorry about that," Everest murmured softly in Mia's ear, his expression apologetic. She clutched his hand tightly, feeling a twinge of fear and uncertainty. With each passing moment, she wondered if she would fall victim to their thirst. She was the lone human amongst these creatures, and the knowledge left her feeling both vulnerable and intrigued.

"Man, Everest, you weren't kiddin'—she looks just like her!" the man with the accent exclaimed.

Mia snapped her head upwards, a bewildered expression crossing her face as she looked at Everest. Unlike him, the other men seemed to lack a filter, openly voicing their observations. *Oh, would they love Lucy.*

"Wh-What?" Mia asked Everest.

He looked at her momentarily, concern flickering in his eyes. "I need you all to leave. I'll see you at the show."

The three men nodded and grabbed their belongings, making their way towards the door. As they passed Everest and Mia, she couldn't help but notice Tommy's eyes flicker brightly again.

"Man, cut that shit out! There's a bottle in the kitchen for ya, ya thirsty fuck!" the man with the East Coast accent reprimanded Tommy, raising his voice.

Despite the stern words, Tommy kept silent and continued walking. "Sorry about that, miss. I'm Robbie, by the way, and that there is Alex—and freak eyes over here is Tommy."

Robbie extended his hand towards Mia, greeting her with a cordial smile that revealed his sharpened fangs. In contrast to Everest's muscular build, he was lean and toned, with dark brown hair that gracefully draped over his shoulders. He wore a simple black long-sleeved thermal shirt with the sleeves rolled up, revealing an array of tattoos on his arms—a colorful assortment of art against his olive skin. She accepted his handshake, her expression polite but curious. He was more rugged than the others—beautiful to observe in his own way—but nothing compared to the vampiric beast beside her.

She immediately noticed Everest did not seem pleased by the interaction. His gaze was fixed on Robbie with a mix of concern and unease.

Noticing Everest's displeasure, Robbie lifted his hands. "Alright, boss. We'll see ya soon."

The room was silent as the three men left. Mia looked up at Everest, raising a brow in question, a slight smile curving her lips. "You're in a band?" she asked, her voice edged with sarcasm.

Everest smirked. "You already knew this, Amelia," he said, slowly ushering her out of the room.

She wandered the halls of his gothic domain, noting his silent observation of her every move. It was dark as she walked forward, her path lit only by the surrounding candles. Her eyes moved quickly over each frame and picture hanging on the walls, noting the many cobwebs and particles of dust that had settled within the art. Once they reached the end of the large passageway, he guided her to a room—where her eyes opened in surprise.

Large black drapes swept across the double-paned windows that surrounded much of the room. A view of the hills beyond lay before her. His bed, neatly made with only the finest green plush velvet, sat before this beautiful view and hardly looked touched by any hands, if at all. He kept his clothing neatly tucked into a wooden wardrobe, and a large wooden desk lay on another side of the room, barren except for a single framed picture. His preference for art—seemingly by the hands of those who could evoke themes of nature or the macabre—was evident in the works framed and hung upon the dark wood walls of his bedroom. It was simple, yet extensive. But the beauty he put into every detail, she thought, was breathtakingly pleasant.

"You don't sleep in a coffin?" she joked lightheartedly.

Carefully turning his head, he scoffed at her inquiry.

"If I decide to rest, on some occasions... I find the bed much preferable, as you will see."

A small, amused smile tugged at her lips as she acknowledged his words with a nod. Curiously, she began to move around the room, taking in the details of her surroundings, though her eyes remained transfixed on a small gold frame that adorned his desk. Inside the frame was an old photograph.

Her mind felt slightly foggy, faint bits of vertigo swirling through her brain as she closely examined the vintage photo. A large man with long dark hair—seemingly Everest—sat on a wooden chair, his face worn and stoic. What caught her attention, however, was the woman standing beside him. Her hair was neatly pinned back, her dress draping to the floor around her, and her hand rested gently on Everest's shoulder.

It was most certainly the Haunted Woman—and the resemblance to herself was uncanny. Her confusion deepened as she tried to make sense of the vision that flickered in her mind. Closing her eyes briefly, a wave of vertigo overcame her, only to be replaced by a vivid image of herself standing beside Everest. She was clad in the lavish gown, its velvet fabric hugging her frame, her hand resting softly on his shoulder. A fleeting flash illuminated their faces before the vision vanished, leaving her puzzled.

"Is this me?" she asked with unease, turning to face him. "Is that why I feel confused? Are these visions truly mine?"

He moved slowly towards her, gently raising her chin with his hand, her soft eyes filled with a desperate need for answers as they met his.

"Yes, little doe, I believe so."

***

Everest had graciously cooked for her, which was surprising given his vampiric nature. In over a hundred years, he had not forgotten his culinary skills, and the meal he prepared for her was one she would not soon forget—a mouthwatering steak paired with flavorful vegetables, accompanied by a rich merlot. Though he himself did not dine, she noticed him pouring a glass of thick, crimson liquid.

He caught her curiosity. "It's blood. We have it by the bottle here—much easier to drink from."

As she nodded, she felt intrigued to know more. "I see. So, do you... plan on drinking from me?"

Caught off guard by her question, he seemed amused. "Would you like me to, Amelia?"

She hadn't thought that far, and now a flurry of questions swirled in her mind. "Uhm..." Her words trailed as more thoughts emerged. Would he turn her? *Would he kill her?* "Will... will it hurt? Will I... turn?"

His brows rose as she managed to get her words out. Sensing her anxiety, his large hand pulled her dining chair closer to him.

"I assure you, little doe," he said, slowly dragging his fingers down her clavicle towards her chest, his cold breath brushing her skin, sending goosebumps to ripple up her spine, "though you might feel a pinch, I wouldn't dream of hurting you. You might even find some pleasure in it."

A devilish smile rose to his lips, and she caught a glimmer of his sharpened fangs.

Would he drain her entirely, or turn her so she could never leave? Her chest rose in anticipation, but as she continued sipping her wine, a touch of confidence bloomed within her. Her curiosity stirred at the thought of what it might entail. Her inner knowing nudged her forward, urging her to take the leap. And as she sat there with him, finishing the last sips of wine, she felt a warmth rise between her thighs, her core tensing at the thought of being bitten.

***

Mia stood nervously in the bedroom, her body tense as she waited for Everest's next move. His towering height loomed over her petite frame, making her feel small in comparison. As he stepped closer, both their heartbeats quickened in anticipation. She tilted her head up to meet his gaze, his eyes glinting with a deep, red lust.

"Uhm…" she whispered softly, her sweet, innocent eyes gazing up at him as if asking the devil himself to take her soul. "What should I do?" she asked, her voice laced with uncertainty and anticipation.

"Sit down," he commanded, watching her slowly step back to sit on the velvet bed.

In one motion, his beastly hands tore the belt from the black denim jeans they laced through. The strength of his forearms made her core clench as she bit her bottom lip. Lifting his cotton shirt, he revealed his muscular chest, which shined dimly amongst the candlelight. He stepped forward and gently knelt down, removing her shoes and undressing her, leaving her bare and exposed before him. At her most vulnerable point, all she could do was put forth trust.

Leaning in for a kiss, his rough hands smoothed over her silky skin, soft moans of pleasure slipping from her lips at his persistent touch. As he tenderly kissed her chest, his hand glided down her body, his fingers slowly dipping into the wet lips of her sex. She closed her eyes, her head tipping back as she delighted in his touch, his cool breath causing her nipples to harden while her chest relaxed in the heavy warmth of comfort.

Her breath caught as he dipped his fingers into her folds, giving focused attention to her swollen pearl. He thrusted gently, making love to her with his hand as she arched her back, needing more—deeper and harder. She wanted him in every way. As her hips moved against the rough pads of his fingers, her desire built towards the brink, her swollen bud ready to explode with sensation.

"Do you like that, my little doe?" he darkly whispered against her ear, his soft, cold breath making her nerves tremble.

She whimpered, nodding as she basked in the pleasure.

"Are you all mine, to forever play with?" he asked, his voice low as he continued to gently thrust his fingers into her.

She nodded again, softly whimpering in response to his question.

"Say it," he commanded, his fingers beginning to thrust harder into her.

"Yes," she breathily whispered, the motion of his hand causing her chest to rise.

Everest's face grew cold. "Say it, Amelia."

"I'm yours!" she let out, her body continuously tensing under his touch.

Sensing the quickening of her breath and the trembling of her body, he leaned in and pressed his lips to her chest. In an instant of heated passion, his fangs dipped into her soft flesh, eliciting a gasp from her as a sharp prick of pain gave way to sweet pleasure.

He drank from her, his fangs piercing her soft, milky skin, his bulge pressing hard against her core. She felt an intense connection with him. There was something primal and intoxicating about the act, and she reveled in the sensations that overwhelmed her. In this moment of physical intimacy, they shared a bond that transcended the physical world, and she felt as though she were merging with him in a way that was beyond words. It was a deeply intimate moment, filled with sensations she had never known before.

He pulled away suddenly, lifting his head as the blood from her breast dripped from his mouth. His hand tenderly traced the wound he had inflicted—a symbol of his claim on her body and soul. She now belonged to him. There was no leaving, no way to escape his possession of her.

"You did well, little doe... See? It wasn't so bad." Everest slyly smiled.

She felt the lingering bite on her chest as her hand traced the droplets of blood that had trickled onto her skin. Nodding in understanding, the pain from his bite seemed to heighten the intensity of her climax, leaving her open to the possibility of experiencing it again.

Grabbing her hand, Everest pressed his lips to the dark liquid quickly beading down, his eyes glowing an effervescent red with every taste of her fresh blood.

"My sweet Amelia," he murmured between kisses, "my obsession. I have waited many moons for you."

Everest leaned up to undress the rest of his attire, his erection bursting free the moment he unzipped his jeans. Mia noticed the head of his cock dripping with precum, his balls tight and full, ready for release.

Leaning back, she opened up for him as his monstrous body moved closer. He nuzzled her neck, tenderly kissing her skin as his swollen shaft rubbed against the wetness of her sex, making her core ache for him to enter.

"Tonight though, little doe," he coldly growled against her neck, "I'm going to make you feel the way you make me feel. I'm going to make your body scream."

Her breath hitched as he entered her, his mouth crashing against hers as he thrust with deep, hard strokes. He would destroy her from the inside out, possessively claiming her until her last breath.

Mia screamed his name, her nails digging into his back as his length worked into her, his tightened balls slapping against her core. Lifting her legs, he buried his cock deeper, creating a dent in her cervix.

As she felt herself come undone beneath him, the walls of her sex pulsed around his shaft, causing heat to flood through her veins. Mia felt another sprinkle of stars pour into her soul, her nerves alight with pleasure. In that moment, Everest deeply groaned, once again spilling his seed into the far reaches of her cunt.

Their sweating bodies lay enmeshed in a sea of unity, the smell of sex and musk permeating the air, Everest's long hair sticking to their skin. He continued to kiss her with heated passion, intent on claiming her many times throughout the evening.

Time seemed to stand still as they spent hours wrapped in each other's arms, exploring the deepest crevices of their souls with tender touches and caresses. In the soft embrace of the plush velvet duvet, Everest held Mia tightly, gently running his fingers through her hair as he listened intently to her stories—*at least, of this life.*

She confessed to him her ghostly tales, always believing there was more out there than what met the eye. Yet no one believed her, especially not about *the Haunted Woman.* He listened closely, looking into her eyes and watching the way her rosy lips moved with each word, though he never gave away any expression that hinted he knew of this ghostly woman's presence—or, rather, *this past life soul.*

While she questioned whether his vampiric powers had a hand in it, the muscles of his face never moved. He merely observed her as she spoke of her human world, occasionally curving a smile when her eyes met his.

He spoke little of his life, more interested in hers. His air of mystery fascinated her, and she could see he was a man of action rather than words.

As her eyes began to grow heavy, she rose from the bed and walked into his adjacent bathroom. Mia was taken aback by the large ensuite tub, the black marble flooring, and a stained-glass window depicting the night sky, with a red moon glowing brightly.

As she marveled at the magnificence of the master bath, her head slowly turned towards the mirror.

Was it her? Or the late ghostly woman—*wife of Everest Steele*—of which her soul tied to?

The mirrored face looked very much like Mia, though she certainly did not have her hair pinned back, nor was her bare body laced in a velvet green gown. Her eyes blinked at the reflection—only to receive the exact motion in return.

Curious, Mia moved her hand, watching the woman do the same.

"What the hell?" she quietly mumbled under her breath—only to see the reflection utter the words as well.

It was clear Mia and this woman were one and the same, and there would be no escaping this fate. Learning to accept the unusualness this new life had brought would be her only option.

Quickly leaving the room, she crawled back under the covers into her vampiric lover's arms.

It may be strange, she thought, but the company beside her made her heartbeat heavily in comfort.

***

As the morning sky rose over the horizon, Mia stood by one of the large bedroom windows, her eyes gazing into the deep forest that lay far below. She had awakened alone in the vampire's bed, assuming he did not sleep and was elsewhere in the house. After tidying herself, she took a moment to admire the quiet beauty that surrounded her—an eerie stillness within the nature of his garden and the distant forest. He had created a landscape, green and lush, filled with an array of flowers, mostly red and white in color.

Throughout her observations, Mia noticed not a single breeze against the trees, not a bird in sight, or any form of life for that matter. But as minutes passed, the large black goat she had noticed the day before slowly walked by, his head down as he grazed on the grass before the window. *Billy*, as Everest had told her, must have sensed her watchful eyes, for his head lifted, the intensity of his gaze glaring directly towards Mia, his mouth slowly chewing on the green grass beneath him. *There's something strange about him*, she thought, her eyebrows raising in peculiarity as he continued to lock his eyes onto hers. But after what seemed like minutes, the mysterious goat continued walking, passing by the window to graze amongst the garden.

Mia turned her head, for the ceiling-high windows stretched throughout the room. As the goat disappeared from view, around the corner, a large beast walked by—half man, half goat. Standing well over eight feet tall, his hooves thundered outside as he moved past. His chest was covered in rich black hair, and he wore black breeches that ended just above his thickened calves. His muscular physique added to his imposing stature, and in this monstrous state, his exquisite horns had doubled in size.

Mia gasped at the sight of him, stepping back and bumping into the velvet drapes against the wall. *This place is filled with monsters*, she thought, fear igniting in her chest. What was she to do—run to her vampiric monster? Quickly leaving the room, she went to find Everest, hoping he would calm her frightened nerves.

The gothic home was quiet, but slivers of cloudy daylight peered through the windows, offering faint light to this blackened cave. Unable to find Everest with ease, Mia walked down the elongated hall they had ventured through the night before, only to hear the gentle sounds of a strumming guitar and the sweet melody of a deepened voice singing softly.

A door was partially opened, and Mia peeked around the corner to see Everest sitting on a large leather chair in what appeared to be a library, another beautifully hand-crafted window with forest views behind him.

He was writing a song, she observed, as he quietly sang harmonious words, taking moments to write down the poems that came to his mind. She had never heard him sing before, and what tenderness his deep voice could produce. Her eyes filled with wonder as she watched him in his study. Though her soul felt hypnotized by the sweet sound of his song, the thunderous footsteps she had heard outside came crashing down the hall behind her. As she turned around in fear, her back bumped against the wall. The monstrous goat, Billy, laid a hand upon her shoulder.

"Ah, you must be Miss Amelia," he said, his deep voice bellowing throughout the hall.

Mia froze with fright, shocked that a goat was speaking to her.

With a heavy swallow, she slowly nodded, feeling puny amidst this giant.

"Don't be afraid, dear. You can go in," he said gently, the beast's hand gesturing towards the study.

As the two entered the room, Everest's head rose from his guitar, quickly noticing Mia's uneasiness.

"Found this one hiding in the hall," Billy said, a soft grin curving against his mouth.

Everest lightly chuckled. "Come," he ushered, waving for her to walk forward.

Mia hastily walked away from the beast. She could handle ghosts—and now apparently vampires—but seeing a monstrous goat-man with horns double the size of her head was something she would have to get used to. Mia wondered if Billy was the devil himself. *Were there more creatures like him?*

Everest gestured for her to sit on his lap, placing his hand around the small of her back. "I see you've met Billy," he said, his eyes glowing a deep red.

Mia nodded. A prickle of vulnerability ran through her chest in the presence of these two beastly giants—*oh, how she felt so small.*

Dragging his fingers along her cheek, Everest sensed her unease. His cold touch sparked a feeling of comfort within her.

"Don't worry, my little doe. He wouldn't even hurt a fly… would you, Billy?" Everest turned his gaze towards the goat-man, flashing a sly grin, his fangs gleaming in the dim light.

"I suppose I wouldn't," Billy agreed, a touch of mischief in his voice.

The three of them shared breakfast together under Billy's suggestion. Mia was at a loss for words watching the beastly creature cook her a meal, which, to her surprise, consisted of foods she ate in her human world—eggs, bacon, and toast. As they ate, Everest calmly sipped from a glass of red liquid, and Mia relished every bite of the delicious meal Billy had prepared. Her gratitude was evident in her expression, and the goat-man looked pleased with her appreciation.

"He's alright," Mia whispered to Everest, a warm smile gracing her face as Billy cleared the table.

Everest smirked at her comment, giving her a nod. "That's why I keep him around."

A moment of contemplation passed through her mind, and her curiosity was piqued. "Are there more of you?" she inquired, her tone steady but with a hint of determination—a sliver of desire to uncover the secrets that may lie beneath his surface.

His eyes flickered—just for a second, barely enough to notice—but Mia caught it. A hint of something concealed, something dangerous.

He reached for her hand, his grip gentle but firm, his thumb tracing slow, deliberate circles on her skin. "I think," he murmured, his voice low and thick with unspoken menace, "you'll find there are far more of us... lurking in the shadows."

Chapter 6

Tending to a quiet demeanor, it was difficult for him to express his innermost pain. With music, he found a realm through which he could relay his sorrows, and it was through this music that he would show his wounds.

"Do you want to go to this with me?" Mia asked Lucy, holding a printed flyer for Everest's upcoming show in Lavender Hill. He had casually mentioned it as he dropped her off at home, handing her the flyer and insisting she must go. With a stern demeanor, he made it clear he wanted her there, and as she intended to obey his words, she hoped to bring someone with her—at least the only friend she could think of.

Lucy looked at the paper in Mia's hands, her eyes lighting up at the printed words. "Oh yeah, that looks rad! Let's go!"

Mia knew Lucy would be thrilled about the show, as she had previously shown great excitement for the band. However, there was another piece of information Mia needed to share—something she had been keeping to herself until now, causing her anxiety. She knew she needed to reveal it soon.

"Hey... where did you get this?" Lucy asked with skepticism.

"Lucy..." Mia hesitated, noticing her friend's quick look of impatience. Her eyes drifted over and saw that Jack was behind them. Steering her away from their boss, she pulled Lucy aside.

"What's going on?"

"I have to tell you something, and you can't say anything," Mia whispered over the loud music.

"What? What is it?" Lucy's eyes widened in eagerness.

"I've been seeing Everest."

Lucy froze, her face showing a mix of surprise and uncertainty. Fearing a negative reaction, Mia couldn't tell whether she was simply shocked or actually upset. After a few moments, however, the punky blonde burst into laughter.

"WHAT?" Lucy yelled with a smile of disbelief.

Quickly shushing her, Mia turned her head to make sure Jack wasn't listening.

"It's a long story... I'm—I'm not ready to explain, but... yes."

Lucy opened her mouth to speak and, for the first time, fumbled for words. "How the fuck did you do that? Every woman in town has wanted that man, and you just moved here!"

"I know... I—I don't know, he came into the store and..."

"I can't believe this shit. YOU'RE going out with Everest Steele?"

"Well... it—it really hasn't been that long. Please don't say anything about this. I just wanted to tell you since I knew you'd find out," Mia pleaded.

Lucy was dumbfounded, her eyes wide with disbelief. "I can't believe this," she said, shaking her head. "You just moved here, and he instantly gets eyes for *you? Well jeez, I don't think I'm that bad-looking.*"

"Lucy, I—"

In the drop of a hat, Lucy's bewilderment vanished as her lowered eyes looked up to Mia.

"Do you know what this means?"

"What?" Mia asked hesitantly.

A slow, mischievous smile curled on her lips, her pearly whites shining against her red lipstick. "Can I meet the band?"

***

As Mia approached the new venue, *Blue Midnight*, she could hear loud music blasting from within the brick structure. The black walls and blue neon lighting gave it an intimidating appearance, making the place seem exclusive. Strangely, there were no people or a bouncer in sight, despite the sounds coming from inside. Confused, Mia wondered if she had come to the right place, but the music confirmed her suspicions.

She hadn't heard from Everest in several days, and to her surprise, she found herself missing him—despite barely knowing him. Her heart was growing fonder of this mysterious, vampiric man. The more time she spent thinking of his haunted nature, the more memories of his past—their shared history—would come flooding in. Memories that were becoming second nature, a not-so-strange reality after all. Lucy kept asking her incessant questions at work, but Mia made sure to keep his private life *private*, disclosing only a reality that would seem appropriate for this world. Lucy ate up every bit of information, desperate to know more about him, especially opening her eyes at Mia's stories of their intimate affairs. Lucy was jealous but could handle the truth of Mia's words and took hope in the fact that there were three other members of Vampiric Hell she could ogle—*if not more.*

"Damn, you look hot!" Lucy exclaimed as she approached Mia from behind. The punky blonde was dolled up, wearing thigh-high lace-up boots, a white low-cut tank top, and a red plaid mini skirt. In contrast, Mia had picked out the most revealing dress she could find—one that hugged every curve of her body. The dress was nearly floor-length, and her long brown hair cascaded down her back. Her rosy lips shined against her subtle makeup.

"Everest is going to shit when he looks at you!"

Oh, how Lucy had a way with words. Mia laughed at her comment. "Thanks, I hope he does."

"Come on, I think Jack's inside. Let's go see what's going on!" She quickly grabbed Mia's wrist, hurriedly dragging her inside. Mia's heart began to race as she tried to keep up behind the hasty girl.

Dampness fell onto Mia's face the moment they opened the club doors, the extreme warmth of bodies permeating the air. The small space was filled with a dark muskiness. The opening band played their hearts out, loud music blasting through the vicinity. It seemed as if everyone in town had crammed into the venue. As bodies pushed through each other, Mia and Lucy stood near the door, unsure of where to go.

Feeling a nudge on her arm, Mia looked up at Lucy, who was gesturing towards the bar.

"I'll be right back!" she yelled.

Through an infinite sea of people, Mia couldn't spot Everest anywhere. *He must be backstage,* she thought. Scanning her surroundings, she spotted someone get up from a bar table leaning against the back wall. She scurried through the crowd, snagging the table before anyone else could. Though packed with people around her, her view from the tall bar stool was clear enough to see the stage. She hoped Everest would spot her quickly. As she scanned the venue, Mia noticed an array of women near the center stage, their bodies dancing to the music in scantily clad attire. Her intuition told her they were all there to throw themselves at Everest. She would not be jealous but would find it difficult to meet their angered eyes *if and when* they see he only had sight for her.

As the minutes passed, Mia spotted Lucy holding two cocktails, aggressively pushing people aside as she made her way towards her.

"It's hot as fuck in here," she yelled, placing the drinks onto the table. "I hope you like vodka."

The drink was strong, with just a splash of cranberry juice. "Thank you!" Mia yelled back at her. Lucy nodded in agreement.

"Where is Jack?"

"At the bar. Gotta watch him though—he gets really drunk sometimes." Lucy tilted her head, trying to spot Jack's activities.

Mia listened to the opening band's performance, unimpressed by their lack of harmonies and the overall chaotic sound. It reminded her of the amateur bands she had seen back in her youth. Almost an hour had passed since their arrival, yet there was no sign of Everest. However, as the time drew closer for the band to go on, a flood of women made their way towards the front of the stage—a seemingly endless sea of scantily clad groupies. Mia took note of the overwhelming number of female fans, which looked to be most of the town, all here to see *Vampiric Hell*.

As the lights lowered, the band finally walked on stage, Everest thundering in last. He wore a green t-shirt with his classic black jeans, his long dark hair wisping against him as he walked forward. His impressive stature seemed to loom even larger in the cramped space, and every woman in the room hung on his every move, their gazes fixed intently upon him, yearning for just a single glance from his sharp eyes. The low lighting of the club cast flattering shadows across his muscular physique, sending a shiver of excitement through Mia's body. She knew he was the reason everyone had gathered here—and yet, he only had eyes for her.

As he approached the microphone, he greeted his fans, the depth of his voice sending shockwaves through the crowd. The ladies in waiting screamed in delight, and while he snickered before them, Mia noticed the slight turn of his reddened eyes scanning the crowd, locking onto her in a moment's flash. A tingling warmth rubbed through her inner thighs as his darkened gaze grasped onto hers through the sea of people. She could feel her heart beating quickly, a rush of blood flooding into her chest as the mere sight of this beastly man controlling a crowd of people gave her core a seeping rush of pleasure.

The crowd roared in excitement as the band began to play, the mass of women at the front continuing to scream in desire. A dark melody loomed through the room, sending a chill up Mia's spine. As Everest's lips graced the mic, the haunting beauty of his voice floated through the air.

In that moment—amid the screaming crowd and the music pouring into her ears—her stomach dropped, and her heart fell into a dazed love she never wanted to end. She was hypnotized by the darkened music, understanding the screams of the fandom around her, but the deep sounds of his eerie lyrics gripped into her being, making love to her soul throughout a crowd of people. She felt frozen in time, the same heating paralyzation as when he first walked into her world in the record shop. Through this hypnotic pleasure, slivers of déjà vu poured into the back of her mind. *This voice was familiar*, she thought, and while the memories were spotty, she knew she had heard the soft sounds of this deep voice sing to her before—many moons ago.

Mia hung onto every word Everest sang aloud, his haunting poetry against the melodic rush of his gothic metal band making her mind drift into an ocean of dopamine, never wanting to leave these waters of bliss. The music felt personal—a deeply hidden reality only she could understand. While the packed room ignited in their own screams of pleasure, she could feel his songs being sung just for her. His haunting lyrics of pain, lust, and desire were words only she could understand, as they were over a hundred years of his inner thoughts.

"Man, these guys are so fucking good!" Lucy yelled over the music, abruptly waking Mia from her trance. She smiled, acknowledging Lucy's enjoyment. They *were so fucking good,* and she could quickly see why the entire town had packed into this small venue. Their dark melodies were filled with metal and gloom, and the voice of Everest Steele was deafening—like Satan himself singing a sad ballad of death.

As the temperature in the already crowded room started to soar, Everest removed his wet shirt, revealing his muscular chest glistening with sweat. He was well aware of the power he emanated in this confined space, and the women surrounding him went wild—shouting and reaching out desperately for even the slightest touch of his towering frame, their hearts yearning for him with a sense of desperation.

Mia slowly bit her lip, knowing far too well how his large presence had pleasured her behind closed doors, while Lucy's eyes maddened like the rest of the women, her mouth agape at the half-naked man on stage.

As the screams of the women fed the monster's ego, he gave them pennies back with a small snicker, which they hungrily devoured at the sliver of attention. He continued to sing his eerie melodies, and as his sharp eyes glanced over the crowd, he quickly winked at Mia, causing her chest to flutter in surprise and her cheeks to blush.

But oh, did everyone notice his every move. The small act caught the room's attention, and the women up front all turned around, squinting and frowning, determined to see who had received this most coveted wink.

Sharply snapping her head, Lucy pursed her lips. "You're fucking kidding me, right?"

Mia smugly grinned, raising her brows in satisfaction.

Her mouth agape, Lucy shook her head in denial. "What the hell, I can't believe this!"

The show continued on as the crowd roared at every song that played. As the end drew near—the final ballad of the evening—a stumbling Jack found his way through the masses towards Mia and Lucy. Slamming a beer bottle onto the table, he placed his hand forward to keep his composure.

"Hey guys," he loudly spat out. Mia couldn't help but notice the stark change in the man she knew at work. The cheerful, well-groomed, easygoing persona he usually portrayed had vanished—replaced by someone who was clearly intoxicated. Behind his blurry, clouded eyes, Mia could sense a troubled soul, secretly masking his woes with pleasured poisons.

Getting up from her seat, Lucy grabbed Jack's arm to help him stand.

"Jack, you're drunk. Are you going to do this every time we hang out?" Her tone was serious as she looked deeply into Jack's tumbled eyes. As Mia observed the two of them, she sensed an energy that extended far beyond their relationship at the record shop.

"Oh shh! I'm just having some fun." With unknowing strength, he pulled her in close, taking his hand to pat her hair.

Displeased with his actions, Lucy quickly pulled away from his grasp, a look of concern on her face. "Okay, buddy," she said, nodding and patting his back with an uncomfortable grin.

Slightly swaying as he held onto the table, Jack turned his eyes towards Mia, who gave him a thin grin in response to his unpleasantly drunk presence.

"Mia," Jack said, reaching out to touch her long hair. "You look fuckin' hot!" He smiled lazily, grabbing his beer for another sip.

Mia looked at Lucy, whose expression instantly turned to anger. Slapping his arm, she yelled, "What the fuck, Jack!"

With a drunken smile, he turned his head towards Lucy. "What? She does! Come on, Mia, I see the way you've looked at me." Giving her a wink, he continued sipping his beer, smiling at Mia through his drunken haze.

"Jack, stop! You're being a creep!" Lucy shouted, slapping his arm again.

Seemingly unbothered by Lucy's anger, Jack set his drink down and attempted to place his hand on an uncomfortable Mia, who was unsure of what to do.

"Hey!" a deep voice thundered from behind them.

Mia looked up to see a towering Everest standing behind Jack and Lucy, his face scrunched in serious concern. As the two turned around to face the beast before them, Lucy's eyes widened in surprise, while Jack remained unfazed in his drunken state. As anger grew in Everest's eyes, his monstrous frame grabbed Jack by the collar, causing Jack's beer to spill onto Mia. The crowd around them quickly turned their attention to the heated scene unfolding in the back of the venue.

"Don't fucking touch her," Everest growled quietly in warning, his glowing red eyes mere inches from Jack's face. A look of terror washed over Jack as he stared into the cold, darkened eyes of the vampire who held him in a firm grip. "She's mine," Everest added, growling possessively.

Abruptly dropping Jack to the ground, he cowered before Everest.

"O-okay, man, whatever you say," Jack stammered, raising his hands in surrender.

Everest snarled, glaring as Jack scurried away from the girls. Around them, the crowd chattered beneath the venue's stereo music.

"Damn," Lucy muttered under her breath, overcome with a mix of shock and realization. "I need a man like that."

Mia chuckled at Lucy's amazement.

"Are you okay?" Everest asked, taking Mia's hand in his. The feeling of his rough palm against her skin warmed her chest in arousal the moment their touch collided. The mere presence of the large beast towering before her in concern caused her cheeks to blush in rose as she sensed several jealous eyes upon her.

"Yes, I'm alright," she assured him, her wide, innocent eyes glimmering as she raised her gaze to meet his. Despite her words, Everest's face remained clouded with concern, his displeasure evident.

"It was just some spilled beer."

Everest sneered, seeming more upset about the interaction than she was. "I don't like him. Come, let's go," he grumbled, ushering her off the bar stool.

"Hey, wait a minute!" Lucy exclaimed in anticipation.

"Oh!" Mia realized, causing Everest to turn back around to face her. He raised an eyebrow at her inquiry.

"Lucy would like to meet the band," she said, her voice softening into a gentle plea.

"Ugh, sure. The guys should be outside."

"Oh, hell yes!" Lucy said enthusiastically. Everest, however, narrowed his brows at her granted request.

Leaning against the venue's brick wall, the three long-haired men stood beneath the pitch-black sky. As they chatted amongst themselves, they raised their heads when Everest approached with the girls.

"This is Robbie, Tommy, and Alex," Everest stated to Lucy, whose eyes glimmered with flirtation as she approached the band members.

"Boy, they're cute," Lucy leaned in and whispered to Mia.

Taking a long drag of his cigarette and dropping it to the ground, Robbie brushed his hand against his pants. "Hey, how's it goin'? I'm Robbie," he said, reaching his hand out to Lucy.

Wearing a black button-down shirt with the sleeves rolled up, Lucy immediately eyed the tattoos on his forearms. As someone usually quite extroverted, Mia noticed the anxiety now bubbling within Lucy. Giving her a slight nudge, Lucy quickly snapped out of it, stepping forward and flirtatiously rambling to, unbeknownst to her, the three vampiric musicians.

"She talks a lot," Everest whispered into Mia's ear. She let out a quiet chuckle, nodding in agreement.

The men smiled at Lucy's words, boosting her ego as she continued to flirt her way into their minds. Mia wasn't sure if they were just being polite or genuinely enjoyed her attention, but as Lucy continued speaking, she noticed Everest lean into Robbie's ear, whispering something inaudible as Robbie hummed and nodded.

Carefully observing the interaction, Mia watched with growing curiosity.

"Heya, Blondie, I'll be right back. Come on, Tommy," Robbie said, pulling him away from the group.

"Oh, okay. So anyways..." Lucy continued rambling to Alex, who seemed slightly confused by how fast she spoke.

While Lucy kept talking enthusiastically, Alex appeared lost, and Everest looked increasingly disturbed. Mia, however, quietly kept an eye on the situation, noticing Robbie and Tommy walking away. Then, further down the road, she spotted their boss Jack slumped drunkenly on a bench.

Puzzled by the situation, she watched as the two men approached Jack with smiles, saying something she couldn't understand. They then hoisted him up to his feet and started walking down a dark alley, Jack's disoriented state rendering him oblivious to what was happening.

Mia pursed her lips at the observation. "What are they doing with Jack?" she asked, looking up at Everest with unease.

His stoic face didn't move a muscle as he looked into her worried eyes. Placing his hand around her waist, he said calmly, "They're just taking him home, little doe. Nothing to concern yourself over."

Mia wasn't buying it, continuing to look at him sharply. She wouldn't say anything now, swallowing her tongue but also afraid to know the truth. "Alright, if you say so."

He took her home, leaving Lucy enticingly thrilled amongst the three large men, who didn't seem to notice Everest and Mia's departure—clearly only interested in obtaining a musician. Of course, their exit wasn't easy, as many fans clamored for a snippet of Everest's attention. He was cordial but slightly uninterested. The crowd of women who had screamed for him inside now seemed ragingly jealous, glaring at Mia as they watched Everest take her hand and lead her away. In such a small town, this man was a star. Yet, they barely knew anything about him.

Mia was thankful to be home after the eventful evening. Though she knew Everest was upset over Jack and remained calm in his presence, she had been soaked in beer, feeling sticky as the black dress she wore clung to her.

"I'm going to take a shower. Jack spilled quite a bit of beer on me," she said, tearing the damp garment off.

Everest's eyes were filled with a fiery intensity as he watched Mia undress and disappear into the bathroom. As minutes passed, the room filled with steam from the hot shower. Mia began to lather herself with soap, feeling a heavy gaze upon her.

"Let me help you with that," Everest said lowly.

Mia looked up to see him completely undressed, ready for her. His large presence barely fit into the compact room, and she felt the heat within her chest rise as she opened the shower door for him, their bodies meshing within the small space.

He lathered her back, massaging the soap against her milky flesh. The touch of his rough hands made her close her eyes, letting out a small whimper of pleasure. She leaned back into his touch, able to feel his pressing erection hard against her. He pulled her in closely, cupping her wet, supple breasts. She moaned at his gentle touch, and he leaned in, softly kissing the side of her neck, his long hair sweeping across her shoulders. His hand moved down her body, into her sweet folds, his erection nearly bursting as he dipped his fingers into her wetness. While she delighted in the steaming pleasure he gave her, the cock pressed against her backside made her core soak at the thought of his release.

She turned to face him, her hands slowly trailing up his muscular form, feeling each dip and contour that shaped his mysteriously alluring physique. The cascade of water droplets from the showerhead made his stone-like frame gleam, creating a mesmerizing effect. Her gaze met his heavy-lidded eyes with desire, the arousal between them palpable in the hot, steamy air.

As he leaned in to kiss her, she held onto his throbbing cock, gently stroking it and rubbing the soft pads of her fingers against his swollen head. Everest let out a groan as she worked his bursting shaft. To his surprise, she cheekily smiled against his kisses, biting her lip as she leaned down, placing herself on her knees while the shower continued to rain down on her.

His sharp eyes watched her every move as she slowly placed her honey-rose lips on his swollen tip, drops of precum already forming. She took him in slowly, her hand working his elongated shaft as her mouth moved to milk him, his eyes glowing hot as he slowly pumped into her, claiming her throat. Her tongue swirled over his bursting cock, and he grabbed onto her hair, directing her movements, her eyes smudging wet from the shower and the thickened cock thrusting into her throat.

"My little doe," Everest lowly growled, his elongated canines gleaming in a devilish smile, "you were made for me."

A whimper escaped her as his cock continued to nuzzle against her lips, his rough hand still grasping her hair with slight intensity. Just when she thought he was going to release into the swells of her throat, he forcefully pulled her off him, swooping up her thighs in one hasty motion and carrying them out of the shower towards the bedroom.

Their bodies meshed in wet lust as Everest threw Mia onto the bed, his massive length thrusting into her as he passionately kissed her through each deepened stroke. Mia yelled his name as her sharpened nails scathed his back, the hard cock deep within her making her core explode with each pound into her cervix. With a loud groan, his milky seed poured into the depths of her, their bodies panting in electrified energy, still drenched in water from their heated shower affair.

He delicately dried her body, carefully cleaning and en-suring that her soft skin was left pristine—exactly the way he liked it. She took comfort in his gentle actions, knowing they portrayed a side of him usually hidden beneath his stoic demeanor. Snuggled against his hard frame, with the soft fabric of her duvet bringing a pleasant tingle to her flesh, she found peace within. Any memories of the past the universe brought forth would not bother her now, for she knew they were meant to bring them together. As she lay there tethered in the arms of her beloved, their resting bodies entwined in a sea of adoration, Mia turned her head, her gaze falling upon the reflection in her bedroom mirror. Staring back at her was a visage of her former self—but this time, she was calm, unbothered by the specters of her past.

Chapter 7

He contemplated allowing her into his hidden world of darkness, where his friends lived—a life concealed behind society's veil. He secretly yearned for her acceptance, hoping his friends would welcome her as he had adored her. He wondered if she would cower from the fearsome beings that haunted the woods. Deep down, though, he dreamed of her embracing the shadows, and someday soon, being able to live freely amongst the creatures that called the night their home—a home, especially with him.

The moon illuminated the midnight sky, and a light wind drifted through the air as Mia headed towards the cemetery the following evening. Her hands were tightly tucked in her jacket pockets, and her hair softly blew against her face as she looked down, watching her steps glide across the concrete. She wore a short floral dress, her bag in hand, and hoped no one would spot her walking to the graveyard this late at night, seeming certainly out of place.

Under Everest's suggestion, he had invited her to spend the evening with him and his friends, giving no specifics except for her to meet them promptly amongst the dead at midnight. She longed to spend her time with him, as she could feel the intensity of their bond growing by the day. His words held power over her, and she would spend any moment she could in his presence—wherever that may be. She only knew a small part of his life, hidden deep within the woods, and his invitation would provide her with more insight into a world cast away by humans. She understood that the monsters lurking in the shadows were real, and while the thought was terrifying, her soul pulled her towards him, unsure where he might lead her.

Standing at the cemetery gates, the breezy air fell silent. As the minutes passed, small flutters of paranoia entered her mind, uncertain of what to expect.

Is this the part where he finally kills me?

"Shut up," she quietly muttered to herself, trying to brush off the fear of the unknown. Her intuition told her she would be alright.

But I'm alone in a cemetery at midnight.

Her ear twitched as Mia heard a low rumble down the road. A large black van slowly approached. Slightly uncomfortable, she took a step back as the vehicle neared, hesitancy rising in her chest as she wondered—was this ride for her?

The door opened, and the scent of musk and patchouli quickly flooded her senses as four large men in black poured out of the van—the last one being Everest. As her eyes adjusted, she quickly realized he had brought his bandmates, all of whom politely greeted her. Everest's large stature unfolded from the vehicle, his eyes burning red at the sight of Mia.

Something's different, she thought, noticing the energetic aura surrounding the four vampiric men. Their eyes were a deeper red than usual, a sense of hunger veiled behind their minds. Mia looked at Everest with uncertainty, though he showed nothing but lustful elation upon seeing her.

"My little doe," he whispered, his rough hands smoothing over her dress, his lips eagerly attending to hers. "I missed you."

His immediate attention brought a rush of heat to flare within her, tingling arising between her thighs. Whatever they had been doing prior had stirred a more restless version of the quiet beast she had known.

I'm not complaining, she thought.

"What are we doing here?" she asked as he continued to trail kisses along her neck, unaffected by those around him.

As he held her close, his large fingers pressed into her soft, thick curves, and his eyes glowed with lust.

"Alex has to get his girl, and then we'll go."

"Wait, what?" Mia asked, her face contorted with confusion.

She followed his gaze towards the cemetery, spotting Alex walking towards a mausoleum, his long leather coat swaying with each step. Her eyes locked onto him as he neared the door and knocked. The name "Jones" was engraved above the entrance, leaving her in a silent state of bewilderment.

"Hey baby, it's me. You ready? We gotta go!"

Baffled, Mia looked up at Everest, his fangs gleaming wickedly, a saucy smile glowing under the moonlight.

"I'm coming, I'm coming!" The mausoleum door blew open, and a petite woman walked out. With green skin and a purple-haired bouffant, she stood on the steps with one hand on her hip, gazing down at Alex.

"Don't rush me! You know how long it takes to look like this?" she said. She wore a black pencil wiggle dress and matching black pumps. Mia stared in shock at the seemingly deceased woman.

How is this possible?

Placing his arm around her waist, Everest leaned into Mia's ear.

"Come on, let's go," he said, ushering her towards the van.

The group crammed into the vehicle, which, to Mia's surprise, was more spacious than it initially appeared. Lined with black leather seats on each side, Mia took her place beside Everest. As her eyes wandered around the van, she narrowed her gaze at the shadowy figure sitting in the driver's seat but kept her thoughts to herself.

Huh, that's not strange at all...

The deceased woman sat across from her, and Mia noticed that beneath her green skin were deep, rooted scars, which, she thought, looked incredibly painful. Yet, this woman masked her wounds with a carefully detailed aesthetic; red painted nails, neatly long and rounded, and her makeup styled like a Venusian beauty, with long, thick black lashes. Though bizarre, she was beautiful, Mia thought.

"Are ya gonna keep starin' or are ya gonna say hello?" the woman asked sharply, her eyes fixed on Mia. She had an accent similar to Robbie's, but her voice was high and shrill—*like one of those old Hollywood films,* Mia thought.

Startled, Mia lightly shook her head and smiled. "Sorry, hi," she said nervously.

Leaning in, Alex nudged the woman softly. "Be nice, Lina. You know who that is," he whispered, though in such close quarters, Mia heard every word.

The woman's eyes lit up at Alex's comment, a mischievous grin growing on her face.

"Oh, I do... You're the dead wife, huh?" she said bluntly. "Doesn't look too dead to me!" She laughed at her own remark, while Robbie and Tommy suppressed quiet chuckles in the back.

Mia had no words. This woman clearly didn't have a filter.

Reminds me of someone else I know, she thought, glancing towards Everest for assistance as agitation grew on his face.

Shooting her a menacing glance, Alex nudged the woman's arm again.

"Lina!" he hissed through gritted teeth, his eyes glowing with intensity.

"Oh, stop, I'm just having some fun!" She reached out her hand towards Mia. "It's nice to meet you, honey. I'm Lina Abigail Jones."

Vibrantly charismatic with a crude sense of humor, Lina was much more than a chatterbox. She spoke faster than Lucy—which Mia could hardly believe—and as she rambled about local gossip within their underground world, Mia stared at her intently, trying to make sense of whatever this woman was talking about. Lina carried a flask in a small hand-held purse, from which she would take swigs from while laughing at her own stories. The guys seemed mildly interested, and Mia found herself wondering how this woman ended up with a gothic vampire who played the drums.

"Alex says she gives really good head," Everest quietly whispered into Mia's ear. She slowly turned her face towards him, a closed-lip grin forming as her cheeks flushed a crimson rose. She tried not to laugh.

The air was cold and biting as the group exited the van. The dark sky loomed above, its inky blackness resembling an endless sea. The crisp air was thick with the scent of fresh mountain pine as they approached the imposing gothic cabin ahead. Though she didn't know what the night held, a strange sense of security washed over her—knowing Everest was there. She stood alone, a mere mortal amongst creatures of terror, yet something deep in her bones whispered she was safe—safe with him.

Feeling a soft brush against her skin, she looked down. Everest had gently taken her hand, ushering the group inside.

I thought there were two of them? Mia thought as she neared the front entrance, noticing only one gargoyle perched high on the roof. With pursed lips, she decided to keep the observation to herself.

Glasses were raised in celebration, filled with a thick red liquid, while Mia watched Lina stumble around the kitchen, opening cupboards until she pulled out a large bottle of vodka.

"Come on, honey! You don't want what they're having!" Lina beckoned Mia to join her, pouring two glasses of vodka. "It's just a little bit of booze, have some!" she said, handing Mia a drink with a playful smile.

"You know, it is so nice to have another girl around. Most of the time it's just me and these crazies." Lina rolled her eyes, taking a long sip from her glass.

Mia laughed at Lina's dramatic flair. "Cheers to that!" she said, raising her glass. Hesitating, she searched for something to say. "So... how did you meet Alex?"

"Oh, you know, he was just running around that cemetery one night and I saw him. He was such a charmer—and so handsome! You know, you always hear stuff about vampires, but I really liked him. Beats going out with a demon or any of the other guys around here. I tell ya, some of these guys are on such a power trip. The last guy I dated thought he was hot shit because he could turn into a dragon. Oh whatever, I'm dead—why would I care about that? I just want somebody to love me, and that's my Alex. He's such a sweetie."

At a loss for words, Mia blinked slowly, taking a long sip of her drink. Hoping the dissociation would wear off soon, she gathered her thoughts. *This isn't a dream. This is real. Nothing is shocking anymore, Mia.*

"Oh... how... nice. So, there's more of you?" Unsure if she was asking the right questions, she quickly realized Lina knew *a lot about a lot of things around here—far more than Everest had revealed.*

Lina raised an eyebrow. "More of us? Sweetie, this is *Heathen's Creek*—don't you know?"

Sensing the confusion in Mia's expression, Lina loosely grabbed her wrist.

"Oh, honey," she said empathetically, frowning and scrunching her face in displeasure. "Everest hasn't told you much, huh?"

Taking another large sip from her glass, Mia shook her head.

"Yeah... he tends to do that. He just bottles everything up! Quiet little devil, isn't he..." Her eyes trailed over to Everest and the other vampires drinking together. "What did you think? That they all lived underground or something? They had to put them somewhere!"

"Them?"

"Oh, you really don't know anything at all?" Lina asked, her voice filled with amused disbelief. "Oh... it's okay. You'll find out soon." She rubbed Mia's shoulder sympathetically. "You know, the more I look at you, the more you look just like her!"

"I'm sorry, what?"

"Everest's wife, you know, you're the one who came back to be with him? I mean, we all know. Hell, Everest has been waiting your whole life. It was only a matter of time!" Lina kept drinking her vodka, babbling away to Mia's growing disbelief.

"Excuse me? *Waiting?*"

"Oh yeah! Didn't you know? I mean, I'm sure you must've known—you're the one who decided to come back! He knew right away the moment you were born. I thought it was kinda creepy, but those psychic powers of his..." Her words trailed off as she continued drinking.

As bizarre as the situation was, an uncomfortable panic began to rise inside Mia. She had always felt a deep sense of safety around Everest—as unexplainable as it may be, but the vampiric man was quiet, never alluding to much. If what Lina said was true, and Everest had known her fate for years, what else was he hiding? Of course, he had already sensed the worry blooming inside her.

She felt a hand wrap gently around her shoulder. Looking up, she found Everest seemingly quick by her side.

"Everything alright?" he asked quietly.

Mia downed the rest of her drink, swallowing her anxiety with a dash of vodka. "Yes," she exhaled, setting the glass on the kitchen counter. "Can we go somewhere a little more private?"

Everest raised a brow, curiosity flickering in his eyes. "Why, of course, little doe."

Grabbing her hand, he led her down the hall towards his bedroom. Behind them, the group's laughter echoed drunkenly through the halls, a maniacal chorus fading the farther they walked.

The house was dark and musky, lit only by dim candles like the ones she had seen before. They cast flickering shadows on the macabre paintings along the walls. Whether it was the alcohol or something else, uneasiness bubbled in her chest with every step. She felt small—truly small—for the first time. A mortal amongst monsters of the night. Her soul still whispered she was safe, but her thoughts had begun to scatter.

When Everest opened his bedroom door and led her inside, her heart beat a little faster.

"Are you alright?" he asked, his eyes glowing faintly red from the bottled blood he had been drinking. She could see concern in his gaze but didn't know how to ask what she needed to. *Would he be upset? He's never been upset with me before...*

He stepped forward, his towering frame casting a long shadow. She instinctively stepped back, bumping into the wall behind her. A wave of anxiety crashed through her as her wide, frightened eyes locked on his.

"Have you had too much to drink?" he asked softly, brushing her cheek with his thumb, the rough pad grazing her lips. Her chest beat rapidly as she carefully nodded, her eyes still locked onto his.

"Your heart is beating very quickly," he stated, sensing the tension in the room. "Pent-up energy? I can help with that..."

His voice was low, and as he leaned down to press his lips against hers, her back straightened against the wall.

"What are you going to do with me?" Mia whispered.

He stopped, his eyes blinking open. "I'm sorry?"

"What are you going to do with me?" she asked again, this time a little louder.

He raised an eyebrow in question.

"L-Lina said you've known about me this whole time. You've known what's been going on, and you haven't said anything."

His eyes darkened, a slight edge of anger forming beneath his stoic expression.

"You never tell me anything! She said you've known about me my whole life, that I was supposed to come back for you. I've spent years in fear, thinking I was being haunted by some ghostly woman who would never leave—and you knew about this? I didn't know who she was! And now you appear, and I'm constantly confused by déjà vu. And the dreams and visions... are you doing this to me?"

He continued to watch her as she spilled her drunken words, her heart racing at his lack of emotion.

"So this is my fate? It was always my fate to live amongst monsters, hidden away? To come back here, reincarnated as someone's long-lost love?"

Her face was flushed with worry as she looked up at him, demanding answers.

He stepped in closer, but she couldn't move, trapped against the wall. A glimmer of sadness flickered in his eyes. *She was his long-lost love. Was that such a bad thing?*

"Is that what you think of me? A monster?"

With a hard swallow, she asked, "What if I choose otherwise?"

Realistically, she had been enjoying her time with Everest Steele. She did not want to leave him; *her heart surely wouldn't let her.* But what would that entail? Potentially giving up her human world, *becoming a vampire? Who would miss me though? Mom? She's drunk most of the time...*

"My little doe," he muttered, his large hand enveloping her face, his gaze fixated intently on her.

The worry etched in her eyes threatened to spill over into tears as she bravely met his stare. She knew there was no escape, no way to change the course of fate. She didn't want to run, but fear had taken hold—years of hauntings and confusion bubbling to the surface.

All she could do was meet his burning red eyes, the tears of her terror mirrored in their depths.

"While I have always known of your presence, I cannot change fate. This is not my doing."

His hand lightly brushed over her beating heart.

"Your soul has decided to come back for *me*," he whispered viciously against her, his chilly breath sending a parade of goosebumps across her skin.

She felt flushed at his words, his large frame causing her heart to pound and her inner walls to clench, his hardening length pressing gently against the silky fabric of her dress.

"But I will say," he continued, pressing his lips against her neck, his hand beginning to trail under her dress, "you were mine the second your soul took this body."

Feeling the wetness seeping through her folds, he thrust into her. A gasp escaped her lips as his fingers pumped into her core, and all she could do was lean her head back against the wall and endure the heightened pleasure—her worries dissolving.

In moments like these, she did not care. She would always give in to his touch, for her soul craved it and nothing more.

If this was truly her fate, she would surrender to his being, for the stars above had written this story moons before her first breath.

Some people enter this world with inherent destinies, but she had been destined for a world haunted by her past—confused and afraid with no explanation, the stars hoping she'd one day find him again. And when she did, a sense of peace would bloom between them. A pain the universe had carried long ago would finally settle through two darkened souls.

She would always be his, without choice, for if she chose another path, the darkness within would only grow deeper. She would never escape the Haunted Woman—the essence of herself, rooted in anger from a life not fully lived. Not fully, *with him*.

His vampirism knew this, and he would never let her go.

But how long could she live like this, in her mortal realm? When would he give her the kiss of death?

Heat flooded her veins as he continued to kiss her, his fangs pressing hard against her flesh.

Nudging her legs apart with his boot, the hardened cock pressing against his jeans was ready for her. She was his obsession, and it was paramount he claimed her at any waking moment. She was to never forget where she came from—who her being belonged to.

Trembling beneath his touch, Mia felt shivers race up her spine as the cold breath of his kisses swept over her skin.

His cock sprang free from the prison of his jeans.

He would have her right there, up against the wall, the monstrous size of his body trapping her within the realm of his pleasure.

As the root of him pushed deep into her cervix, she moaned into his mouth, her blood pulsing, lost in sensation.

Lifting her thighs, his swollen shaft possessively pumped into her, her hands gripping him as she bounced against his thrusts—her back hitting the wall with each hard claim.

He was feeling greedy and would not stop, burying himself in the depths of her core, making sure she would once and for all remember everything—that this was her fate, and she was to never question it again.

As she felt the intensity of his thrusts—*his emotion, his pure essence*—her eyes closed, her intuition knowing she had made love to him in years past.

Slivers of memory flickered through her: the way he touched her in another life, the way he made her explode into stars. Her inner walls pulsed against his length.

Gasping, Mia's head hit the wall as a charge of electricity flowed through her veins, her earthly orgasm spilling through her body.

Everest groaned as he released his seed in a tight embrace.

As she opened her eyes, her breath caught—

The ghost of her former self stood just behind Everest, her hazel eyes glowing and staring intently.

And in the next blink, she was gone.

Though the truth of her past life was now clear, Mia realized the apparition would never leave. The woman's brief appearances would always remind her of a story left unfinished—a heart broken by a death too soon.

"Where are we?" Mia asked as Everest gently placed her on his bed.

He looked at her curiously. "We're in my bedroom, little doe," he said, a soft smile on his lips.

"No, I mean what is this place? Lina said there are many more of you... What are you hiding?"

He knelt down before her, taking her hand and pressing his lips against her skin.

"I'm not hiding anything, Amelia."

"So what is *Heathen's Creek*?" she asked skeptically.

Looking at her for a moment, his eyes began to glow beneath a knowing smile.

"Come, I'll show you," he said, nodding towards the door.

Chapter 8

He never wanted her to see his true identity, for beneath his snowy flesh lay a creature that could kill. Only in his most raw moments did the creature emerge, and he used all of his strength to keep it hidden away.

"Boy, you guys had some fun!" Lina yelled with a saucy grin as Mia and Everest walked back into the kitchen. The three vampiric men next to her chuckled at her outspokenness.

"So, are we heading out soon or what?"

"Yeah, I'm ready to go," Alex agreed, looking towards the rest of the group.

"Where are we going?" Mia whispered to Everest as the group began to grab their belongings and head towards the front door.

Placing his arm around her, he tugged her close. "To town—there's a party going on."

Mia grew concerned, her face a mixture of worry and doubt.

"It's okay, little doe. You'll be safe with me. I said I'd show you around."

As the group walked deep into the woods, Mia could feel the chilly mountain air pressing against her skin, a shiver racing through her as she continued into the black midnight. She was unsure of what was to come, but Everest grabbed her hand, the touch of his palm against hers bringing a sense of comfort as they navigated the unknown. The rest of the group had walked ahead, stumbling in laughter through the evergreens, while Lina was still swigging from her flask. Mia knew they were heading towards *Heathen's Creek*, assuming it was a place hidden away from the world, filled with things and creatures she dared not dream of.

"So, what is this place?" she questioned again, holding tightly onto his hand.

"This is my home," he said as they continued walking into the darkness of the forest. She was unsure how far they had to go, as she could see nothing but the dim moonlight casting shadows through the trees.

Heathen's Creek was his home, his *haven*, he explained to her. Few people knew that the dark entities and creatures from stories existed in the real world as well, kept hidden away by authorities many moons ago. As the years passed, they were slowly forgotten, so they created their own world where they could exist freely. After leaving his previous life, he ventured west—alone and unsure of his place in the world—now a being with a thirst for blood, a killer, an outcast, a *monster*. And through that long trail of loneliness, hiding in the shadows, he heard word of Heathen's Creek.

"So I came here, and I've never left. I built my home on the outskirts; I like the privacy of the woods."

Mia appreciated his openness, knowing there was pain he had held onto for decades. He was clearly a man of solitude, but he needed his mate most of all. Her heart filled with sorrow—an intuition of his deep pain—and a sense that she was not only living through that pain but also inflicting it. She could feel the memories of the past slipping into her mind in fragmented glimpses. She couldn't change the past, though. The universe wanted her soul to return for him. And now here she was, and her heart told her never to leave. *Not that she had much of a choice.*

As they continued walking, Mia saw dim lights appear in the distance, and the faint sound of laughter carried from the direction they were headed. Lina, Alex, Robbie, and Tommy raced ahead, leaving Mia alone, holding hands with her Everest Steele. As they reached their destination, she turned to see a large wooden sign nailed to a pine tree. The words were written in smeared red ink: "HEATHEN'S CREEK." She shuddered, wondering if the ink used was actually blood.

Clutching his hand tightly, she looked around, feeling a sense of unease building inside her as the reality of this hidden world of monsters began to sink in. Still, she clung to a glimmer of hope, trusting that Everest wouldn't harm her. Despite her concerns, his friends seemed good-natured enough, and as her gaze took in the surrounding scene, an ever-growing sense of trepidation rippled through her chest.

"It's okay, *Amelia*," Everest assured her softly. His simple words were calming, but the underlying uncertainty within her was much louder.

A hidden village tucked deep within the chilly forest, Heathen's Creek was a secret haven for monsters of the underworld. This was no fairytale, but a place where society's darker creatures dwelled in obscurity, shielded from human eyes. Brick and wooden structures dotted the landscape, their glow enhanced by candlelight. The nocturnal commotion of the central area filled the air, and soon her eyes adjusted to the sight before her. Creatures that could only be thought of as mythical were casually chatting with one another, living their lives in blissful harmony.

Demons, Mia noted, dressed in black velvet with polished boots, their curved horns protruding from glistening red skin. She knew it wasn't right to stare, but she couldn't help it as she walked past a pair standing outside a pub with drinks in hand, their sharpened teeth gleaming in candlelight smiles.

She was unsure of the hour, but the village was livelier than any ordinary town on any ordinary day. Suddenly, a loud thud behind her caused her heart to sink as fear gripped her senses. She clutched Everest's hand tightly, desperately seeking reassurance.

"Don't be scared, little doe," he chuckled lowly as she held onto him. "He won't hurt you."

As she stood there, mesmerized and terrified, a colossal dragon thundered by, its crimson and onyx scales reflecting the light and dazzling her eyes. Nearly as tall as the towering trees within the forest, the monstrously oversized creature moved past them, causing the ground to tremble beneath their feet. Despite Everest's attempts to reassure her, she stood frozen in fear, her breath catching in her chest, unable to comprehend the sight before her—or shake the growing sense of terror that consumed her.

She couldn't believe what her eyes had witnessed, yet not a soul batted an eyelash, each minding their own business while her vision was bewildered by the monstrosities before her. *How do you hide a dragon in the woods?* she wondered. *Are there more?*

As the village center bustled with the jovial spirits of darkened entities, Everest continued to introduce Mia to his world, pointing out the many shops and businesses that ran within Heathen's Creek. Her mind drifted to the fairy tales she had read as a child, teeming with all sorts of life. But the atmosphere in this realm was profoundly different, tinged with a menacing energy that lurked behind the seemingly cheerful laughs of its inhabitants. A sense of danger lingered; darkness was concealed beneath the surface.

"Is it always this busy here?" she asked Everest as they continued to walk down the central road. An endless party of chaotic festivities, the streets ran wild with howling noises and creatures running mad throughout the road, pushing past them.

"Yes," he nodded at her inquiry. "We like to stay up late... as you can tell."

"Creatures of the night..." she muttered to herself, her words trailing off as her eyes glazed over what looked to be a large orc walking his three-headed dog.

"Cerberus!" the towering orc angrily bellowed to his furry beast, hastily pulling the animal away from sniffing a bystander. *You don't see that every day...*

"It's right up here," Everest said, pointing towards the end of the main village road, where a line of pines scattered off into the near distance.

"I wouldn't trust him!" shouted a raspy voice, startling Mia. She turned her head to see an old witch leaning against a shop door. Wrapped in a black cape, the woman's body was awkwardly hunched, supported by a wooden cane. Above the storefront, a plaque read Apothecary. Peering into the darkened space, Mia could only see a deep well of shadows behind the witch.

"He's hiding something from you. You're in grave danger!" the woman raspily hissed at Mia, waving her cane towards her.

"Excuse me?" The woman looked absolutely mad—her body nearly in decay, her face withered in extreme age, with sunken gray eyes. Her words came out harsh and bitter, but Mia always wondered if any of her anxieties held even a sliver of truth to them. Her soul felt safe with Everest, but he *was* a vampire, and deep down, she did question whether she was truly out of harm's way amongst him, his friends, and his world. She was still a human, and the thought had crossed her mind multiple times. *What would he eventually do with her?* If they were so-called lovers across time, would he not turn her for his benefit? Which made her wonder: *Why would this old woman say that?*

"I see you, vampire!" she hissed again, glaring up at Everest with angered intensity. "You cannot fool me!"

Baring his fangs at the decrepit witch, Everest puffed his chest and told her to back off, his eyes a burning red sea of rage.

"Come, Amelia, let's go." Quickly pulling her away from the witch, Everest stormed off in haste, Mia running to catch up with his thunderous strides.

"He controls you!" she faintly heard the witch yell.

"Everest, wait!" Mia cried out behind him, her breath catching from anxiety and adrenaline. "What was that?"

Finding a quiet spot near the end of the road, he turned towards her. "Don't listen to her. Those old witches are delusional."

"B-but she..." Her words were quickly cut off by the fury in Everest's eyes. She had never seen him look so upset.

Yet, *if what the woman was saying wasn't true, why would he be so mad?*

"Don't listen to her," he growled. "Come, let's go. The others are waiting."

Swiftly pulling her arm again, she stayed silent, pondering the witch's grim words in the shadow of the vampire before her. He had always been kind and gentle, but the energy that now lingered in the air felt different. Something was off—a side of him beginning to show that she was uncertain of. Vampires, as she knew, were always predators. She had been delighted to spend every moment with him, as it felt right within, but *what did the inner workings of his mind truly have planned?*

***

At the far reaches of the village, the occupants of Heathen's Creek would gather for lustful play. They had created a place for those who wished to partake in fantasies of their maddened desires—more endless partying and overall debauchery. Only those with the darkest minds tended to emerge and entertain the evils of the hidden realms within. Thus, they created *Hell's Paradise.*

Deafening music emanated from the two-story black stone building at the edge of the forest. Partygoers were scattered outside, beers in hand, some collapsing to the ground from their drunken states. She heard laughter and screaming, and moans of pleasure whirled through her ears as she looked to see a dark-haired woman with wings pinned to a wall, being railed and thrust into by a minotaur. Her sharp nails scratched the hair on his back as he forcefully rutted into her, their minds lost in their sexual play—and no one around seemed to mind at all.

She wasn't sure what to think. *Why would he take her here?* She assumed it was to show her everything about his life, and what that contained. But as they had walked the streets of the village, watching the lively enjoyment of the locals, this felt much darker—this felt *unsafe. Is this what the witch meant?* She continued to hold onto his hand, feeling smaller by the moment as they walked forward towards the entrance, the music and maniacal laughter growing louder with each step. She noticed she hadn't seen a single human since arriving at Heathen's Creek. *Was she the only one here?* She hadn't received any strange looks, but she wondered if she should be feeling more guarded.

Everest wouldn't hurt her—*he said so*—but what if this place of mindless debauchery caused one's inhibitions to disappear? *What if this was where it all ended?* She looked up, and a large satyr stood nearby, a drunken mess with a bottle in one hand and his exposed cock in the other. Creepily smiling, he attempted to stumble towards her, though Everest quickly pulled Mia away, baring his fangs at the creature who had intended to have his way.

She felt frightened. *Why would he bring me here?* She clung to the witch's words tighter with every step forward—but also to his hand.

The dimly lit club filled her senses as she stepped inside. Red lights flashed in time with the heavy bass pulsing around her; the once-muffled sounds of music now overwhelmed her ears. A hot, stifling heat enveloped her, and the scents of red wine, roses, and incense filled the air, creating a strangely pleasant and calming effect.

A sea of bodies filled the space, and as her eyes adjusted, she quickly noticed the many creatures now surrounding her in close quarters. Some were standing, enjoying drinks and dancing, while others pleasured each other on plush velvet couches.

"Billy got us a table in the corner," Everest yelled in Mia's ear. "The others should be there too."

Mia nodded, still gripping the rough flesh of his hand. She felt unsure of herself, but all she could do was hold onto him as they moved through the crowd, telling herself he was safe. Even if her heart believed it and her mind was unsure, it didn't matter. In this moment, in a room full of monsters, he was the only one she knew—the only one to protect her, *she would hope to believe.*

They continued to push through the crowd, Mia tightly clinging to Everest's arm as he led the way. Squeezing past the dancing bodies, their sweating skin, fur, and possible scales brushed against her. Through the endless sea, her eye caught a glimpse of the main stage. Red lights illuminated several pole dancers, bare-skinned, their red-toned bodies glowing beneath the lights. Their horns protruded from waist-length hair, and they radiated a sexual confidence and beauty Mia could never dream of possessing. Their demonic energy was alluring, and those up front delighted in watching the appetizing bodies dance with lustful grace before them.

She quickly scanned the scene, her eyes widening. Taking center stage, a nymph straddled a werewolf. The muscular monster gripped her thighs as the purple-haired woman slowly grinded against him, her dark wings sparkling vibrantly, her nude body glistening beneath the red lights as she moaned with each thrust. Her eyes shut in bliss, beads of sweat slowly dripped down her center onto the wolf's thick fur. A shocking sight—yet something within Mia wished she could exude the carefree confidence these creatures had. It wasn't in her nature, but she wondered if Everest had ever been on that stage—or what he would do to her if given the chance.

"There you guys are!" a bellowing voice called out as they approached a long bar table. Billy, whom Mia had briefly met, stood up from his chair to greet Everest. The two of them, side by side, towered in stature, while Mia continued to feel small in their presence.

"Nice to see you again, *Miss Amelia*," the goat man said humbly, his dark eyes observing her as he bowed to press a kiss upon her hand. The contact of his flesh reminded her of the petting zoos she had visited as a child, feeding goats as they eagerly ate from her palm. This was no ordinary goat, though; his muscular body carried no innocence compared to those childhood memories.

"Please, come sit down," Billy urged, waving his hand towards the group.

"Who can we ask for a drink around here?" Lina loudly asked in annoyance, turning her head to see if any staff were available. Sitting across from her, Mia watched the undead woman squirm in her chair, a look of furious desperation on her face as she searched for a waiter. Leaning in, Alex whispered something to Lina, and Mia observed his hand move towards her thigh, quickly causing Lina's tension to ease. A knowing smile appeared on her lips as a fire lit within her eyes. For the few hours Mia had known them, their relationship seemed strange—but clearly, he knew the key to her happiness.

Placing his arm around Mia, Everest pulled her closer, the small act a quiet claim of territory. He leaned in, the cold air of his breath brushing against her cheek, his lips nearly meeting hers when a sudden thud startled her. They both quickly turned to see a gargoyle standing before the table. A black apron wrapped around the stony monster, and a tired look of weathered exhaustion was carved into his face.

"Well, finally!" Lina snapped, bitterness in her tone.

"All right, what'll it be?" the gargoyle grumbled. His voice was deeply raspy, as if stones rumbled in his chest.

Looking next to him, Billy lit up at the sight. "Barry, my boy! How kind of you to stop by—tired of the old roof?" he joked playfully, smacking him on the back.

The gargoyle smirked, rolling his eyes. "Yeah, yeah. It's been a long night," he muttered. "What can I get you guys?"

"Well, I want—" Lina began to yell, but was cut off by Billy's thundering voice.

"How about... a round of shots for the guys..."

"Hey, make mine a double!" Robbie called out. "Type A if ya have it."

"Yes, and some *Sapphire Desires* for the ladies. I'll have a gin and tonic myself." Lina's eyes lit up with excitement. Billy leaned in closer to Barry. "And put it all on my tab. We want to show Miss Amelia here what we're all about."

Barry nodded as he glanced at Mia, who offered an awkward smile.

"Hey, how's it goin'?" he acknowledged. The more she looked at him, the more she realized he looked very much like the missing gargoyle from atop Everest's roof.

"All right—couple a' bloody shots, *Sapphire Desires*, and a gin 'n' tonic. I'll be back in a few." Barry walked off, his stone body thudding away slowly.

"Everest..." Mia leaned into his ear, a sense of peculiarity stirring in her mind.

"Yes, little doe?" His arm remained wrapped around her, pulling her in close.

"What does your other gargoyle do?"

A clever smile grew across his face—she was catching on now. There was a knowing sparkle in her eye as she looked at him.

"Construction," he replied, a laugh escaping his chest.

"Ah, interesting..." she said, nodding in approval. *His demonic land held no bounds,* she thought to herself.

Mia glanced at the drink that had been set before her. A soft layer of smoke rose from the martini glass, and a single cherry sat amidst the blue, smoky concoction. It certainly looked intriguing, she thought—*quite fruity*—but she wondered if there was more than what meets the eye. She looked over at Lina, who was already sipping hers, a relaxed smile loosening her lips with every taste.

"What's in this?" Mia asked Everest with slight suspicion.

He leaned into her ear, his icy breath tingling against her skin. "Magic," he whispered with a smile.

Not the answer she was looking for, but she had expected no less from him. She began to open her mouth to protest when Billy stood up from the table, glass in hand.

"Well, cheers to us all!" he bellowed, raising his glass to the group. "To another night of hedonistic fun... and to our new guest, *Miss Amelia*."

Locking his eyes onto hers, she sensed a hidden energy within Billy he was withholding. As with all those around her, she felt they, like Everest, harbored sexual deviants within—presumably this was where they set themselves free. Feeling the heat of Billy's gaze, she sensed him wanting to devour her, a burning he would let loose if given the chance. Within a flash, he looked away, and Everest never noticed. The group cheered, drinks in hand, and down they went. Mia, however, was still hesitant.

"It's okay, little doe. I'm sure you'll like it—look, Lina does," Everest quietly reassured her.

She looked over at Lina, who had already finished her drink. Her mood had quickly shifted to a state of relaxation, and joy washed over her face.

"Well, cheers then," Mia said reluctantly, raising her glass to Everest.

He clinked his shot glass against hers. As the light essence of smoke billowed towards her, she coughed. But as she took a sip, she instantly caught flavors of berries, vanilla, cinnamon, orange... and something else she couldn't quite put her finger on.

Her vision heightened, her skin beginning to tingle as the music and atmosphere around her intensified. The smell of incense wafting through the club now magnified through her nostrils, causing her mind to slow down. A warm feeling of soft comfort entered her being—she felt relaxed and at peace amidst the chaos.

Her ears perked up to the blaring beat of the bass, the club's music now slowing down in her mind. Placing his hand on her thigh, Everest carefully rubbed the rough pads of his fingers against her bare skin, a pleasurable sensation flowing through her body. Her eyes began to close as her mind wandered, her head lightly swaying to the lustful beat. Feeling Everest place his arm around her, the touch of his skin against hers caused her shoulders to melt into a state of warm relaxation.

She opened her eyes, and Lina was whispering something to Alex. The two stood up and walked away.

She felt at peace within herself, her prior worries now vanished. Not a care in the world could bother her. *The drink was pure magic*—and she had only taken a sip.

Sensing her state of bliss, Everest pulled her in close. His large hand pressed gently against her face, dragging her towards him, his mouth crashing into hers. All she could feel was the soft touch of his lips and a fire igniting within her, wanting to escape.

Feeling the warmth between her thighs, she sensed her body eager for release. As the pleasurable intensity grew throughout her body, she smiled against his kisses.

"What have you done to me?" she murmured, her lips curling in joy as her heart beat faster with every press of his mouth.

He smiled back, a gentle laugh escaping his throat, his cold breath sending more chills up her spine.

With everything around her, Mia wanted the moment to last—her heightened sensations glorifying the pleasure coursing through her. She did not care if others were nearby; her eyes were glued onto him. Her soul truly felt that she had known him in all lifetimes, and nothing else mattered. It didn't matter if he had always known of her existence. It didn't matter whatever the witch had said. Any anxieties she had been holding were now set free. She could not care less in her state of ecstasy.

She felt the duality within herself—a life before that was lost too early, and now a life truly lived. She remembered it all. The calm in her mind brought clarity she had never known before.

This was truly magic, she thought. *Was she in a drunken haze, or were these feelings real?*

"Hi, boys," Mia heard a sultry female voice say.

As she turned her head away from Everest, the group looked up to see two demonesses had stopped by.

They looked nearly identical—thick black horns protruded from their heads—though one had purple, shoulder-length hair, and the other had pink hair cascading down to her waist. Sparkling bodysuits bedazzled their devilish, red-hued flesh. Adorned in gold jewelry, thick plated rings shined upon their fingers, highlighting the length of their sharp black nails. With piercing eyes that glowed like a cat, ready to pounce at any moment, they had now chosen to come out and play.

Candy and Amber, working girls of Hell's Paradise, offered their private services to those in pleasurable need. With a kink for vampires, the twins had an *obsession* with their musical patrons—who, up until now, had always delighted in their presence.

"Hi there, handsome," the purple-haired demon said lowly, taking the lead to sit on Robbie's lap. She slowly caressed her hands up his chest, her nails lightly grazing the soft black fabric of his button-down shirt. "Miss me?" She leaned in for a kiss, but Robbie gently placed his hands towards her, turning his face away.

"Hey, uh, Candy, not tonight. I'm hangin' out with the guys right now!"

Visibly irritated, the demonic woman scrunched her face. "Excuse me?"

"What's this?" the pink-haired demon asked as she stood before the table, her menacing gaze directed at Everest and Mia. She slowly walked towards them, bending down behind Everest and smoothing her hands over his shoulders. "Come on, handsome. Don't you want to play?" she whispered into his ear.

Firmly grabbing her wrist, Everest turned towards the demoness with a look of anger. "Go away, Amber. I'm not interested." His darkened eyes grew shades of red as he stared intensely at the demon beside him.

"Since when?" she hissed, attempting to rub her hands against him again.

Mia felt nervous. An uncomfortable energy lingered throughout the group as the demonesses continued trying to seduce their way into the laps of the vampires. While she didn't care if these were the women he'd spent time with before, she was more concerned with how a demon would react to rejection and disappointment.

Quickly standing up, Everest towered over Amber, baring his fangs in anger. "Go away, Amber. I'm not interested," he growled, his voice a thunderous, deep rumble.

Flames grew within Amber's eyes at his denial, her chest rising in heated aggression. Though he was much larger than the seductive demoness, and rage spewed through her menacing stare, she simply snickered at Mia before walking off into the depths of the club's crowd. It was unsettling, and something within Mia told her the twins would be back—they wouldn't give up so easily.

"Oh, don't worry about them. They're always causing trouble," Billy said, breaking the silence that had gathered. "I'm surprised you weren't interested though." He gestured towards Robbie. "You always have a bit of Candy." He winked, a knowing grin lifting his mouth. Robbie smirked, a look of hidden unease behind his eyes as he looked away from Billy.

"I apologize for that," Everest said to Mia, whose nerves had eased now that the demons had left. "Are you alright?"

His hand smoothed over her leg in comfort, the sensation of his touch still tingling from her magical drink.

"Yeah," she said cautiously, nodding as she grabbed her glass to finish the rest of her *Sapphire Desire*. The more she drank, the more heightened her senses became. Though she was in a state of bliss, the brief interaction with the twins left her feeling paranoid. She was becoming keenly aware of her surroundings—trapped in a room filled with monsters and creatures of the night. Her heart raced. She needed a quiet moment, somewhere away from the chaos.

"Is there a bathroom here?" she asked the guys uneasily.

"Uh, yeah—it's over there!" Robbie yelled, gesturing to the far side of the club.

"I'll be right back," Mia said to Everest. He nodded in approval, his eyes following her as she walked away into the depths of dancing bodies on the club floor.

She pushed her way through. Monsters of the night slowly swayed to the sounds of the lustful music. Trying to keep the creeping paranoia at bay, she focused on walking forward, hoping her destination wasn't too far. *Must find the bathroom.* But as she managed to get past the dance floor, her dilated pupils wandered to a stretch of velvet couches. In the corner, her eyes landed on Alex—seated comfortably with his head tilted back, and Lina's face buried firmly in his crotch.

Momentarily frozen, Mia stared from a distance, her chest racing faster as she absorbed the scene, her breath stolen by such a public sight. Lina was knelt down, knees firmly planted in front of her vampiric lover, her mouth sensually bobbing over his large shaft. His eyes were shut, his face locked in ecstasy. She was slow and calculated in her movements. The swipe of her tongue across the thick of his head made his face tighten, biting down on his lip as she pleasured his most sensitive spots. Her neatly manicured hand stroked his shaft while her mouth continued sucking him dry. A tingling sensation danced across Mia's skin, intensifying. A part of her wanted to join in. A part of her, electrified by desire, could feel the wetness soak between her thighs, aching to race back to Everest. But another part of her remained anxious, nervous, and slightly paranoid. *It's not right to stare.* She quickly looked away, and the ladies' room was just ahead.

Pushing the door open, a single fluorescent light glowed above, its brightness causing her to squint. The room was empty, and for that, she was grateful. Walking over to the sink, Mia looked into the mirror and let out a deep sigh, her body still pulsing to the rhythm of the blaring bass just outside. She looked up—and all she could see in the mirror was the Haunted Woman, her old self that would never leave. Would she ever be able to see anything else now? Her reflection was a constant reminder that was tied to a past and an immortal lover who refused to let her go.

Mia continued to stare. Though she could feel her chest rising with each breath, all she could see was the apparition before her. Her eyes locked onto the beaming hazel pupils staring back. She moved her arm, and once again, the reflection mimicked her. Feeling a sudden tightness around her neck, her hand shot up and felt fabric. In a panicked state, she looked down at herself—only to realize the reflection had now transferred to her physical form.

She frantically touched her hair, her neck, noticing the velvet dress that now draped upon her body. Her movements were rushed, disoriented, the mirrored version copying each one. *Was this a trick? Was this magic?* Panic rose within her—and in that moment, the door blew open.

"Well, hello there," a sultry voice called aloud.

Immediately turning around, Mia locked eyes with the demonic twins, who had now cornered her in the ladies' room. Her anxiety surged, and with a quick glance down, she noticed she was no longer in the velvet gown—back to her normal self. *Was that an illusion?* She was flustered, and things were only getting worse.

"Uh, hi," she nervously let out.

They were beautiful, confident—and up close, terrifying. Circling around her, they looked her up and down, curious about what stood before them.

"We don't normally get humans around here," Amber said, tilting her head, bemused by Mia's presence. "*You must be special*," she purred into Mia's ear, her warm breath against her skin sending heat through her nerves, a faint aroma of cherries and bubblegum wafting up her nose.

"She can't be that special," Candy hissed, her brows narrowing at Mia, clearly unimpressed by her mortality.

"Oh, come on, Candy... have a little fun," Amber's voice dropped, thick with deviance. Frozen in uncertainty, Mia remained still as the demonesses closed in around her, the single fluorescent light glaring down into her eyes.

"Are you not afraid, little one?" Amber whispered, her fierce gaze locking onto Mia's unease.

"What?" Mia asked, voice trembling.

Amber laughed, a maniacal chuckle revealing her sharpened fangs. Her lips, full and painted with red-rose lipstick, framed crisp white teeth as sharp as blades. "Oh, little girl, it's such a treat for us that you're here," she said as both demons stepped closer, Mia's back pressing against the bathroom sink. "Look at that soft skin of yours. So pure, so..." Amber slowly raised her hand, her elongated nails grazing just below Mia's neck like a blade, ready to slice its prey.

Tensing, Mia's mind scrambled for an escape. Amber and Candy had her cornered, and their stiletto heels made them tower over her. She could try to squeeze beneath them or shove them aside and make a run for it. They were menacing and toying with her. She knew they could hurt her—but how far would they go? Mia was in their world, surrounded by other monsters and creatures capable of doing far worse. Her heart pounded, sweat beading along her forehead.

But she wasn't quick enough.

Amber's nails dug deep along her neckline, like a knife dragging across her pale skin. Blood began to pour.

I'm not dying today. This isn't happening.

The burning sensation from the cut spread fast. Blood spilled down her neck as she clutched the wound, desperate not to fall. As the demonesses laughed at her pain, Mia summoned every ounce of strength she had and shoved past them. Her hand struck Candy's chest, causing the demoness to stumble in her stilettos. Candy slammed back against the tiled wall, startled and furious.

"Hey!" she shouted, but Mia was already bolting out of the ladies' room, Amber's deep, echoing laughter trailing behind.

The moment she was out, hot, pressurized air hit her skin, and all her senses ignited again. She was still under the spell of the *Sapphire Desire*, but now, there was no pleasure—only raw fear and paranoia. Her neck bled from the deep gash left by Amber's nails. She was shocked they hadn't killed her outright. They liked to play with their prey, tormenting her with fear.

She needed Everest.

Dazed and frightened, Mia darted forward. All around her, bodies moved in a haze of dancing and lust. She shoved past every monster and creature in her path, forcing her legs to keep going, even as her chest begged her to stop. Her eyes caught a flash of something—was that another human?

A small blonde woman, the only human Mia had seen all night, sat on her knees, leashed to a troll.

What the hell is going on? Is that my fate, too?

"Everest!" she cried out desperately as she reached the table, clutching her throat, her hand slick with blood.

The men at the table looked up, startled from their merriment. Mia stood before them—panting, pale, eyes full of tears and horror.

"What happened?" Everest leapt to his feet, concern washing over him. But his eyes quickly shifted into shades of red as they took in the blood smeared on her body.

"The—The—Candy and Amber. They tried to kill me!" she cried, a flood of tears spilling down her face. Frightened and confused, she clung to Everest, burying her head deep against the swell of his chest.

He was her safety. Her only lifeline in the chaos. Only he could soothe her pain and create comfort in a world full of monsters.

Everest's chest rose with anger. He was seething, his eyes a maddened glow. He held onto Mia tightly as her tears and blood soaked into him, and with a knowing glance, he looked at Robbie, Tommy, and Billy.

"On it, boss!" Robbie wasted no time, pushing out of his chair to find the twins. Tommy and Billy followed suit—the large, goat-like man thundered away while Tommy sauntered past, the sight of human blood stirring a thirst in his mind. Everest growled, furious that his bandmate could not control himself. Shaking his head, Tommy backed down, then raced away to find the others.

"What happened, little doe?" Everest asked, kneeling before her.

She was a mess. Makeup smeared, blood and tears splattered across her face as she pressed tightly against her gash. Still under a drunken spell, she wanted to leave.

It was hard to speak as the tears wouldn't stop. "I—I—I don't know. They cornered me, and Amber slashed me with her nails. I—I don't want to be here anymore. I don't like this, Everest. Please... They're going to kill me!"

He firmly held her hand, intently listening to her pleas. "You are safe, my Amelia. I have you here. No one will hurt you. The guys will take care of this."

She nodded, but the tears kept flowing.

"Come. We will leave shortly." Standing up, he picked her up and seated her onto the table for his examination. Looking down, he gently removed her hand and grazed his thumb over the slash of her wound. Her breath hissed in pain at his light touch. She needed immediate care—and he was her only lifeline.

But he was still a vampire, and fresh blood was mere inches away. He didn't want to hurt her. He truly didn't.

His reddened eyes grew more intense, but she told herself he would help—for he was the only one she could trust. She always had, in all lifetimes. Helplessly looking up at him, she waited for his response. Her cheeks and lips were streaked with tears, her doe-like eyes locking onto his, silently pleading for help.

But in this savior moment, he saw innocence—and his thirsting mind needed more. Because of who she was, he always had control. He could buy blood by the bottle. Why would he ever want to harm her? Only in their most intimate moments had he tasted the wine within her—and only at her discretion. But here she was, sitting before him, waiting for his next move. Pain ignited within her, and she helplessly sought guidance.

After a night of merrymaking and drinking the finest plasma around, he was fixated. He was thirsty, and her open wound—freshly cut by the demon's nails—made his eyes glisten at the sight of the sparkling red before him.

He pressed his lips against hers, and while Mia was baffled by his response, her drunken helplessness didn't oppose his touches. They always made her spine tingle and her thighs squeeze. Passionately, his lips smothered hers, her back arching against the bar table as she let him have his way. The club's music still blared in her ears, her mind beginning to slow as she let the sensations ease in—the warm smells of incense and wine continuing to waft through her brain. She felt tired, exhaustion rising within her. Her movements slowed as she absorbed the energy around her and the silky lips of the vampire kissing her.

She could tell he was hungry. He was feisty with his hands, quick to touch the wetness between her sensitive folds, and his lips nibbled over her now-exposed breasts. She felt his long, wispy hair brush against her skin as he hungrily devoured her wounded body. Overstimulated, she felt she had entered a dream—her eyes beginning to close, her thoughts drifting elsewhere.

With surprise, he thrust into her, her cervix pounded by his aching erection. It was pleasurable, but her mind was faint with pain and exhaustion. The fogginess was too much to bear. She couldn't fight him off—nor did she care to. He would always care for her, right?

His cock continued to rut into her, and he whispered his claim into her ear, his eyes possessed with need. Mia blinked—and in that moment, he had changed. What toppled upon her was not the dark, romantic Everest she had known—but a glimpse of a beast. A bat, per se. Large, muscled, and filled with desire. Thick black hair covered the creature, with pointed ears and blackened eyes—claws gripping into her tender skin.

Horrified, her eyes widened—a gasp barely escaping her throat—when everything went black.

He had bitten her. The witch was right.

Chapter 9

He could not explain himself. The monster within needed to claim her, and it was an inevitability he had tried to ignore. He would take whatever consequences were thrown his way and care for her every need, hoping deep down she would not resent him.

"What the fuck, Everest?! What did you do?!"

Her eyes lazily opened; speckles of a cloudy sky peeked through the drawn curtains. It was morning, and Mia could hear shouting in the next room. *What's going on?* She was in Everest's bed, the comfort of his velvet duvet weighing down on her body, and the sound of a woman yelling rang through her ears. *Lina.*

"What do you think is going to happen to her? What will the council say? A human hasn't been turned in years!" Lina's voice shrieked throughout the house. Mia could hear Alex trying to calm her down, and Everest grumbling a few words. *What's going on? Turn a human?*

Mia noticed rather quickly that she wasn't feeling too well. Her mind was foggy from last night's activities. As her head began to pound, a violent illness swept through her. *I'm gonna be sick.*

Racing out of bed, she darted into the master bathroom, vomit spilling profusely from her mouth. She felt terribly weak, as if death had consumed her soul. Never one for too much partying, she wondered how much she had drunk last night, but this wasn't any hangover. Her skin crawled in shivering tingles, and a deep pain cascaded through her body. Her neck felt tender and sore. Breathing deeply, her eyes adjusted momentarily—only to realize she had thrown up blood. Deep barrels of it splattered into the toilet, dripping onto the marbled tile. Mia gasped in fear at the crimson sight. *Is this death? What has happened?*

Trembling, her frail body pushed up from the floor, her heart pounding with fright. She had no reflection. Her eyes glanced down at the pale skin of her hands, tracing the painful wounds along her neck and chest, and as her heart raced with growing intensity... *No...* Small fangs were beginning to protrude from her canines. *Does it happen that fast?* Panic seeped in—but then came a knock on the door.

"Amelia?" It was Everest, and for the first time, the sound of his voice made her heart swell with rage—a new-found fury she could not control.

Opening the door, she met his concerned gaze. Behind him stood Robbie, Tommy, Alex, and Lina, all visibly astonished, nearly afraid of the crazed-looking being before them. Mia was a mess—blood splattered across her body, her hair disheveled, and last night's clothes wrinkled and clinging to her skin. She was breathing heavily, an uncontrollable rage spilling from her bones. It felt otherworldly. Painful. And she wanted to scream.

"What have you done to me!" A dark scream bellowed from her mouth as she rushed forward with sudden speed. Shoving Everest with her newly acquired strength, his monstrous body flew back, crashing into his wardrobe with a thunderous crack.

The group gasped in shock.

"Whoa," Tommy whispered, mouth agape. Lina sharply looked at his dumbfounded expression.

"She's got superstrength. Man, I was sick for a week when I turned."

"Shut it, Tommy!" Lina hissed.

Calmly rising from the splintered wardrobe, Everest dusted off his pants, glaring at Mia with an unreadable expression. She stood before him, radiating fury, a glow of red burning in her eyes—her anger far from spent.

"Little doe," he said firmly.

She was beyond reason. Without hesitation, she grabbed his guitar from its nearby stand and hurled it at him. He ducked swiftly, avoiding the blow, but before he could react, she lunged, pummeling his muscular frame with a flurry of wild punches. Despite the force behind her hits, he remained composed—never retaliating, never showing pain.

Lifting her off her feet, Everest patiently waited for her tantrum to subside. She huffed, glaring at him menacingly.

"Are you done?"

"I didn't ask for this!" she hissed, her words dripping with venom.

"Did you not think this would happen? You are mine, Amelia," he said sternly.

Her eyes blazed with fury as he gently set her down. With a final huff, she spun on her heel and stormed into the bathroom, slamming the door so hard the surrounding pictures and paintings fell to the floor in shattering crashes of glass.

"Well, that went well," Alex muttered sarcastically.

"Man, not the guitar..." Robbie groaned under his breath, pinching the bridge of his nose.

Lina rolled her eyes and stormed out of the bedroom. "Idiots."

As her back hit the door, Mia slid to the floor, tears spilling from her eyes. *What am I going to do?* She knew their souls were intertwined, but the innocence of her humanity hadn't yet connected the dots—she would become like him. Logically it made sense, but they had never truly had the conversation. He found his way into her life—*this* life—consumed her soul and being with everlasting want and emotion, and in a moment's flash, threw her world upside down. *How would she explain this?* To her family? Her friends? She would have to disappear from everyone she once knew, for she could not—*would not*—reveal the secrets of Heathen's Creek.

What family, what friends though? Your mother? She's a rich drunk... and Lucy? Oh, they won't miss you at the shop...

She would now and forever be tied to Everest *in this immortal form.*

At least I won't see any ghosts in the mirror...

She sat there for hours, water continuously springing from her eyes, and with it came another realization: she couldn't just *sleep it off. For fuck's sake*. She could rest, but never sleep again. So, leaning her head back, she closed her eyes and tried to think of nothing. Blanketing her mind, Mia attempted to calm the feeling of illness and rage inside. She felt the need to run, the anger within her wanting to burst out and go as fast as she could. *Is this normal?* she wondered, never having experienced such intense emotion before. She felt awful. She looked awful. But through all the emotion, all she could do was curl up on the bathroom floor, a depression quickly sinking in as she realized she had no more choices. It was only him. It had always only been him. And while her heart still deeply yearned for his, the upsetting truth of the matter was that she had never had a choice. She was to be perpetually haunted until she couldn't leave. *But what's so upsetting? I love him, right?*

The door opened, and Mia could feel the heavy energy of Everest's large frame standing behind her. She had no idea how much time had passed, but in her weakened state, she felt apathetic. She stayed in place, curled up on the floor.

"Little doe, you must drink this," he said, crouching down beside her.

Her eyes glazed over to a chalice placed in front of her. She knew it was blood, but her senses noticed there was something more to it. Her body told her to urgently drink the glass—it needed the liquid to survive—but the thought also repulsed her. Mia sat up, slowly moving her head towards Everest with a sigh.

"Drink," he commanded again, ushering the glass towards her.

Staring at the dark liquid, she slowly swirled the glass in hand, watching the blood slosh around in the clear chalice. She felt a rumble within, her body aching to feed and nourish itself, but her pounding head still felt sick at the thought of drinking... wherever this came from.

"You will feel much better after you drink this, Amelia." He looked at her sternly, a sense of urgency hidden behind his eyes.

Mia eyed him crossly, but remaining silent, she listened to his words. With a sigh, she drank it down, wiping her mouth with the back of her hand.

"Not so bad, right? Now come," he said gently, reaching down to lift her off the floor. Despite her fatigue, she managed to stand. The once-pristine bathroom that had been elegant and grand now resembled a cave, stained with the bloodshed of her transformation. With calm composure, he moved past her to start running a bath.

The warm water enveloped her cold skin, and she felt a sense of comfort as the steam surrounded her body. The sound of the rushing bathwater created a soothing rhythm, easing her thoughts and bringing a sense of tranquility to her mind.

Remaining at ease through every moment, Everest tenderly cared for her as she began to discover her newfound state. The blood she drank had, in fact, helped her pain, and as the thick red liquid poured down the swells of her throat, her inner knowing told her it was his. She was to drink his being to solidify their eternal bond—and whatever she was to become.

He kneeled beside her as she lay in the enlarged Roman tub, the overcast sky dimly shining through the stained-glass window, an array of colors reflecting onto the water. A sea of herbs and rose petals floated around her, the floral scent intoxicating her senses.

"You won't get in?" Mia asked, turning as he attempted to wash her hair.

Her question caught him off guard, and he raised a brow in surprise. "If you'd like, little doe." A thin smile graced his lips as he began to undress, revealing his muscular body to her.

The touch of his fingers massaging her scalp caused her eyes to close, a small whimper leaving her lips. Her head dropped back, and as she leaned against him, his lengthened cock began to grow, rubbing against her curves. He never explained last night's actions and didn't seem to want to, but his caretaking abilities made her heart feel full and safe. She craved his touch. She felt anxious about the future, but the vampirism growing within her made her mind lean into a newfound feeling of power and rage, letting go of the nervous, riddled girl she had been before. If this was always to be her destiny, why be afraid anymore? She was his, *but he was hers*. And if she were to live an immortal life with him and all the creatures in Heathen's Creek, the fire within told her to run wild.

Pressing his lips against her neck, kisses cascaded down the crevice of her skin, his hand moving toward her delicate entrance. Soft moans left her throat as his fingers dipped into her folds, circling her sensitive rosebud. Her heightened awareness enhanced her feelings, and if this was to be part of her new being, she would blindly accept. She rubbed against the thick cock that was hard against her, and her back arched within the warm bathwater, leaning into the touch of his rough hands. Her lips parted—*oh*, how his movements electrified her body. An orgasm poured through her skin. He had bathed her, cared for her, and made sure she was deeply sated, no matter the circumstance.

She was breathless as she turned her head to face him, seeing heavy emotion behind his darkened eyes.

"What now?" she whispered, her chest steadily rising from her satisfied nerves. She turned around, her body straddling him in the bath as she twined her arms around his neck.

Grabbing her hand, he placed a kiss upon her skin, and a soft smile grew as his lips pressed against her body.

"We are to be wed," he murmured, his eyes growing hot with anticipation.

Chapter 10

It would be right this time; she could never die on him now.

It was at his insistence that she wear green, and a hissing voice inside her told her it was the right thing to do. It was *her color*, he had noted—it was *what looked best*. He never once brought up her past self or his past marriage, but he was well aware that Mia knew from dreams and memories. Her vampirism only made the visions stronger, a sort of mind power, *where she could see all*. So, the day had come, shortly after he announced their engagement, and Mia stood before the mirror, depressingly thinking to herself that she wished she could see her reflection.

"Oh, you look just beautiful!" Lina exclaimed as she finished curling the lengths of Mia's hair, the long dark strands falling down her back. She wore a simple veil to match the green lace gown that draped around her, a trail of fabric laced in floral patterns flowing behind.

"I do?" she asked hopefully.

"Honey, he's gonna want to rip this off the moment he sees you," Lina laughed, finishing the touches of Mia's hair and makeup.

The dress was stunning—a deep shade of emerald green that shimmered softly in the dim lighting. As she looked down at herself, she couldn't help but admire the intricate craftsmanship that had gone into creating the gown. A young fairy-like woman—a banshee of Heathen's Creek—had helped her with the design, revealing that it would be a special occasion indeed. The mention of a wedding sparked excitement in the banshee, who shared that it had been a while since a nuptial celebration had taken place in their hidden town.

She wasn't sure who would be in attendance, as her new world revolved around Everest and the few bandmates and friends he brought around. He didn't want her out of sight, and she had to leave everything she once knew behind. *It would be too risky*, he would say—for the paling of her skin and the reddened hue of her eyes easily gave way to a drastic change. *But you go into town?* she would plead, knowing he still went to the record store or played shows in Lavender Hill. He would shake his head, dismissing her pleas. He loved her, but his past pain became prevalent whenever she wanted to do something outside the realms of their wooded home. He wouldn't drive her beyond the forest. She was to leave her human life behind. In a way, she had become his prisoner, confined to the demonic land of Heathen's Creek. But any moments of resentment were quickly filled with memories of contentment and a longing for love.

A smile curled on her rosy lips at Lina's comment. "Yeah," she lightly chuckled. "He's certainly good at that."

"Girl, if I had a body like yours, I'd be wearing much less—but that's just me, and Alex likes..."

Mia's mind drifted off as Lina continued to speak. Her life lately had been a whirlwind, and now here she was on her wedding day, living with monsters and deep forest creatures, abandoning her family and all that she knew. She wasn't sure how long it would take for her mother to notice she was missing—or for Jack and Lucy to realize she'd disappeared from work. Would they post flyers? File a missing person's report? Her mother was a drunk, and there was a high chance she would never notice.

It had taken days for her body to adjust. His strong bite upon her flesh had caused the vampirism in her veins to grow strong, but her small frame became weak with illness as it tried to adapt to this new being. She grew accustomed to drinking blood, and in this modern-day Heathen's Creek, bottle shops and grocery stores made it easy to quench her thirst. Her newly formed fangs—sharpened and pristinely whitened—had not yet dipped into live flesh, *yet*, and she was still unsure about the thought of ever wanting to, for there were much easier ways to obtain the liquid she so needed to survive.

"It's time!" Mia heard an unfamiliar voice say through the bedroom door, Lina quickly gaining excitement and running around the room. She barely knew anyone here, unsure of whose voices belonged to whom. She was a stranger at her own wedding, unclear about who was waiting in the garden for her arrival.

A cold air pressed against her skin as she stepped outside. He had chosen the day of a darkening storm—black clouds hovering nearby, lightning flashing in the distance. His hillside garden was littered with wildflowers, and a wedding had been created within the natural scene. Her heart froze as the many creatures of Heathen's Creek turned to gaze at her, but as she stepped forward, Mia's eyes locked onto Everest, and a warm comfort blossomed in her heart. Walking down the aisle alone, her ears perked up to the sound of an organ playing, and she tried to set aside her nerves by focusing on the groom before her, mindful of the many eyes wandering over the new bride-to-be.

Everest's enlarged frame was fitted into a black suit, the length of his dark hair lightly wisping against the storm's breeze. He held his hands together tightly, staring at her with intent as she approached. He had been waiting a lifetime for this moment—*again*—and his eyes darkened a crimson rose as she neared him, for she would be, forever in his eyes, *his little doe.*

Grabbing onto his hand, swirls of love floated through her chest as she gazed into his eyes. *This is right,* her intuition whispered. *There is no other way.* As the ceremony began, she focused all of her energy on him, pushing aside the pressure of the many monstrous looks looming nearby.

"With this ancient blade, may blood be shared for all lifetimes!"

Thunder roared ominously as the cyclops priest spoke aloud, commanding the attention of all in attendance. Everest's hand took hold of Mia's, slicing her flesh with a sharp knife. She had never witnessed such a sacred ritual before, her eyes wide with uncertainty. Blood dripped from her delicate skin into a crystal chalice, mingling with that of her new husband. Their eyes locked as they drank deeply from the blood-stained glass. When he placed a simple diamond ring onto her finger, her eyes lit up at the sparkling jewel.

Everest's desire burned hot, his hands hungrily claiming their newlywed bond with a kiss as the cyclops declared the ceremony complete. She leaned into his embrace, their mouths intertwined in a passionate, lustful hunger. Cheers and gleeful applause echoed in her ears, the creatures of Heathen's Creek eager to celebrate to the point of delirium. It would be a long night. She would find herself the catalyst for endless revelry, the creatures drinking themselves to oblivion in honor of the newlyweds' union.

The party took on a devilish air as the creatures of the forest descended upon the couple, offering congratulations on their marriage. Mia responded in silence, a sense of bafflement washing over her as she took in the sheer number of monsters gathered. They lavished praise on the vampire groom, who accepted their accolades with gracious nods, never once letting go of her hand. All eyes remained on the pair as they sat in their thrones, surrounded by partygoers dancing and drinking the night away. The backyard of the gothic home had turned into a frenzy of heathenistic activity, the monsters letting loose in drunken madness. The revelers danced and laughed with wild abandon, their crazed merriment filling the air. Dark storms swirled above, illuminating the night with flashes of lightning, sending the creatures into fits of joy. Their howls and cheers blended with the heavy music echoing through the forest. An unholy party for an unholy union.

As the night wore on, Everest leaned in close, his voice a soft murmur against her ear. "Would you care to dance, little doe?" he asked. With a gracious smile, she nodded in agreement.

As his arm slipped behind her back, the music slowed to a gentle pace. She swayed with him as others began to take hold, pairing off in couples for a tender moment. The blackened storm had now settled into thick clouds, and the natural scent of the forest wafted through the air. The very creatures that haunted nightmares now swayed under the stormy sky, embracing the sweetness of a celebration born of love.

We never had cake, Mia thought as she slow danced with Everest, her eyes casually wandering across the décor. *Vampires don't eat cake.* It was a disappointing truth she'd have to adjust to.

"Come, little doe," whispered Everest into her ear. The sounds of the partygoers continued outside as he led his bride away, guiding her into the dark wood interior of their home.

"You look beautiful, Amelia," he murmured, his lips reaching in for a kiss as her back hit the edge of his bedroom desk, the cold air of his breath gliding along her skin, arousal sparking up her spine.

The sounds of the wedding faded in the privacy of the master bedroom. She felt attuned to his desires, ready for him to claim her. Her once innocent eyes now held a sultry red gaze as he gently held her head, their lips meeting in a tender, forceful kiss.

As her hands slipped along the desk, she heard the crash of the single gold frame falling to the floor, glass shattering. Neither seemed to care. Everest held her tightly, his lips grazing her skin, and his hard erection pressing against the lace of her gown. Lifting her onto the table, he rucked up her dress, his hand slowly traveling up the tender insides of her thighs.

In her new form, Mia felt everything with more intensity—the bond between their hearts causing her blood to race, a need that urged to erupt the moment his hands graced upon her body. As he coated his fingers with her wetness, a moan escaped her lips, his digits pushing deep into her core. Eagerly grabbing his cock, she whimpered through their kisses, desperate for more.

"My needy little doe… it's always something," he whispered under his breath, a curving smile breaking through their kisses.

Pulling him closer, Mia laid back against the table, squirming beneath his touch and overwhelmed with need. Lost in sensation, she felt his chilled breath graze her neck as his elongated fangs punctured her flesh.

A loud moan left her lips as she felt him plunge into her, her inner walls clenching tightly around his hard cock as he thrust deep, his teeth biting into her chest. Pleasure seized her. His fat testicles slapped against her with each thrust, and her nails dug deep into his rough flesh. She could hear the fabric of her gown tear as he devoured her body, his cock pounding through her cervix.

Flicking his thick thumb against her swollen bud, her back arched to meet his rhythm. The rough texture of his hand made her nerves ignite. As her orgasm surged through her, her nails dug deeper into his back, her sharpened teeth sinking into his flesh.

They became one. Mouths bitten into each other, her body electrified in passion, his seed spilling deep into her core. She could taste the blood within him—the blood that made her forever his.

***

The brisk morning air carried a cold breeze, a reminder of last night's storm. Mia sat outside, absently watching as Billy grazed in the grass beside her, the sound of busy goblins cleaning up the aftermath of the wedding filling the background. The small yet nimble men and women worked quickly to restore the Steele home to its former state, their speedy efficiency surprising her. *What an odd life,* Mia mused to herself, never imagining this was where fate would take her.

She hadn't laid eyes on her husband since the early hours of the morning; he had spent most of the time partying with his friends, who had now retired inside after an eventful evening.

"Everest!" she called, having spotted him walking near the tree line in the distance. He didn't turn his head, his large frame continuing on, intent on his destination.

Mia raised an eyebrow, puzzled, and slowly stood up.

"Oh, I wouldn't—"

Mia looked down at Billy, who was in his goat form beside her. "Wouldn't what?" she asked sharply.

The goat looked at her blankly, continuing to chew on a straw of grass.

With great curiosity, she quickly took off after Everest, staying just far enough behind that he wouldn't notice. *Where is he going?* she wondered, watching him stride deeper into the woods behind their house. *He must know you're following him...*

A few moments ticked by, and amidst the shaded woods, the structure of a small building came into view. Moss clung to the black bricks, its dark silhouette framed against the dim light shining through the trees. She hid behind an evergreen, eyes glued to the scene as she watched him disappear through the door, leaving her alone. She waited a few tense seconds before cautiously following.

The heavy door groaned as she pulled it open, the metal handle cold beneath her touch. She had grown stronger, but her newfound strength was no match for his. The darkness of the descending stairs made her shiver, and in a moment of clarity, she realized this was a crypt. The fact that he had kept this secret from her raised questions in her mind. *Why would he hide this?* she wondered, assuming this was a place of rest for him. As she stepped forward, the door slammed shut behind her, and darkness engulfed her sight.

Carefully descending the long, dark stairs, her vampiric senses attuned to the eerie atmosphere around her. Slowly entering the main corridor, her eyes adjusted to faint candlelight. In the distance, she could see the flickering glow of candelabras. Soft droplets of water echoed through the air, creating a chilling aura. As she continued forward, she saw the faint image of the Haunted Woman standing at the far end of the shadowy hall, lingering by a set of double doors. However, as she blinked, the woman vanished into thin air.

With a sense of trepidation, Mia approached the entrance, hesitantly grabbing the door handles. Opening them with a quiet creak, she discovered two burial vaults. Rows of candles cast their glow over the empty stone-carved tombs, a deafening silence enveloping the space. *He must be resting here,* she thought as she walked into the crypt. *But what is the second vault?*

Reading his name inscribed onto one tomb, she circled to the other—and her heart froze.

In Loving Memory

Of

Amelia Steele

Devoted wife and daughter

1831 – 1860

What the hell?

Confusion and anger surged through Mia's thoughts. Without hesitation, she used her strength to forcefully push open the lid of the vault. A solid wooden coffin lay inside, its wood appearing new and untouched, as if it had been crafted recently and hadn't aged.

More questions raced through her mind as she pried open the coffin, dust and cobwebs filling her vision. Delicately brushing aside the silk-like threads, she revealed the skeletal remains of a woman dressed in a green velvet gown. Dark tendrils of hair draped over the skull, miraculously preserved through time. A simple diamond ring rested on the bony fingers of the woman's remains.

Mia's red eyes widened in horror at the sight, noting that the ring was nearly identical to her own. She quickly looked down at her hand—her wedding ring had vanished. Her mouth fell open in shock. But before she could fully process it, the skeletal figure lurched forward with a sudden, jerking movement, snatching her with bone-thin fingers and dragging her into the tightly confined space of the coffin.

She gasped as the heavy lid slammed shut with a deafening thud, plunging her into darkness, the chilling touch of velvet and bones pressing in from all sides.

THE END

Thank You for Reading

Thank you for reading the first book in the Heathen's Creek series! I look forward to sharing with you all more stories about the dark entities that live hidden away, and the romance that blossoms between creatures of the night.

Enjoy!

About the Author

Anna Hellström writes horror, fantasy and romance. With an affinity of the shadows, she likes to share her love of monsters and oddities. She lives in California with her husband and dog, and likes to create magic through the written word.

www.ingramcontent.com/pod-product-compliance
Lightning Source LLC
Chambersburg PA
CBHW071115100726
47908CB00008B/2381